S L O W
BURN

Also by Eleanor Taylor Bland

Dead Time

SLOW
BURN

ELEANOR TAYLOR BLAND

ST. MARTIN'S PRESS ---- NEW YORK

Design by Diane Stevenson/SNAP · HAUS GRAPHICS

Library of Congress Cataloging-in-Publication Data

Bland, Eleanor Taylor.
    Slow burn : a Marti MacAlister mystery / Eleanor Taylor Bland.
        p.   cm.
    ISBN 0-312-09237-7
    1. Afro-American police—Illinois—Fiction.   2. Policewomen—
Illinois—Fiction.   I. Title.
PS3552.L36534S55   1993
813'.54—dc20   93-19382
                                                                     CIP

First Edition: August 1993

10 9 8 7 6 5 4 3 2 1

This book is dedicated to:
My aunt, Alica Marchand, March 16, 1899–July 5, 1992
Margaret Kaiser, 92 years young
Leonard Hogan, hero

I would also like to express my appreciation to Joe Nemmers, Chris Turek, and Tom Scott for making my juggling act easier.

For technical assistance, thanks to Mark Blitstein, M.D.; Leo Delaney, Esq.; Erik Eberhard; Charles Homberg, M.D.; Dorene Kuffer, Esq.; Georgina Matthews; Louise Powell; Mike Quane; Greg Schuenemann; Marietta Webb; and a very special thank-you to Warren Wood, senior planner, Lake County Department of Planning, Zoning, and Environmental Quality, for all of his special assistance.

S L O W
BURN

When Janey woke up she was in the closet again. Something was touching her face. Feathers. Must be the woman's dress. She pushed it away. The floor was hard, and it was dark except for little cracks of light at the edges of the door. It wasn't a little closet like the one at home. Didn't smell like mothballs, either. Stank like the woman's perfume.

She couldn't hear anyone talking. Where was the woman? She began shivering and couldn't stop. Her teeth were knocking together. She pulled down a coat to cover herself. Curling up, she wished she were smaller. Too late to be scared. Should have been scared before she got on that bus in Chattanooga.

She pushed the coat away from her face, looked up at the clothes hanging above her head, then moved back until she touched the wall. Feeling around for shoes, she grabbed one with a long, pointy heel. If that woman hit her again, at least she'd have something she could use to fight back.

This door was locked, but she had to figure out how to get away from them when they let her out again. Best to try while the woman was here alone. If she didn't get away, and the man wasn't here, the woman was gonna beat her again.

How was she gonna get back home? Never should have come here. She wanted to live with Maddie. They be just alike, her and Maddie, not smart like her other sisters. She meant to stay with Maddie in Chattanooga. Should have done that. Safe there. Baby-sat them three children for two weeks and got that money and decided she'd rather be someplace else, like a fool. Tiffany Lewis come here last year. All the way to Chicago all by

1

herself, stayed with her auntie for a month, came home with some brand-new clothes none of her sisters got to wear first. Now she come here, she had nothing but trouble.

They were joking her, both of them. The woman joked her when she brought her here, making like she would help her find a job. Now the man would joke her too, making like he was gonna help her get back home. She would have to lie down with him and let him touch her.

A key turned in the lock and the door opened. The light was so bright she had to close her eyes. She held the toe of the shoe tightly.

"Come on outta there," the woman said.

Janey stood slowly, holding the shoe behind her.

"Come out here."

"No!"

The woman leaned into the closet, pushing the clothes out of the way, grabbing Janey's arm and pulling her into the bedroom. Janey brought her hand up and raked the heel down the side of the woman's head. The woman let go of her and cussed.

Janey dropped the shoe and ran, but the woman grabbed her by the hair. She didn't even get to the front door.

1

When Det. Marti MacAlister arrived at the Lakeshore Clinic, the fire was out. Some spectators were beginning to walk away, but many waited, arms folded, talking in small clusters. Children stamped their feet in the puddles of water, laughing and calling to each other as if it were a fiesta.

Marti shouldered her way through the crowd without identifying herself as a peace officer. At five ten and a hundred and sixty pounds, she was what her mother called healthy. People tended to move out of her way. It was a little after eight o'clock. Lights from emergency vehicles lit the night sky. The night was hot, even for July, and humid. Marti had changed her blouse before leaving the house and it was damp with sweat already.

She passed the yellow barricades, avoiding the hose lines from the two fire trucks that remained at the scene. It would be several hours before the building cooled down and the risk of the fire re-igniting had passed. She checked to see if her partner had arrived, but didn't see him. One ambulance was parked near the two-story building, lights out, doors closed. She walked toward it.

The odor of smoke and charred debris grew stronger as she approached. The red brick was blackened above the windows. Water ran from windows in thin streams. Shattered glass was scattered across the sidewalk.

Ben Walker, a paramedic Marti knew, was leaning against the ambulance, his face streaked with soot. His uniform was dirty. Walker was a bear of a man—not fat, just big, with the lumbering grace of a large person who was light on his feet and accustomed to his size. Marti couldn't picture him doing anything as delicate as starting an IV. His nine-year-old son, Mike, was a friend of her nine-year-old, Theo.

Ben gave her a slow smile that began in his eyes. "You're late, MacAlister. Your partner's already around back. He must not be causing too much trouble tonight. The arson investigator on this one doesn't have much patience with people telling him how to do his job."

"Little things like that don't bother Vik." She nodded toward the ambulance. "Think you've got another victim inside?"

"According to the doctor who owns the place, there shouldn't have been anyone in there."

"He still around?"

Ben nodded toward the building. "Saw him go around back. He identified one of the bodies for us. One of the receptionists."

"Dispatch says you found two females. How bad were they?"

"Smoke inhalation. One ran into the closet. The other one was on a table in an examining room. The doors were closed and the fire didn't burn in that direction. Wouldn't surprise me if they both could have gotten out."

"Young? Old?"

"Receptionist was twenty-two. Hispanic. Her mother was here five minutes after the first units arrived. The brother showed up and they both had hysterics until he started hyperventilating and Mom began complaining of chest pains. We sent them both to the hospital."

"And the other victim?"

"Black, looks to be ten, twelve years old. The clothes she was wearing seemed a little odd for a visit to the doctor, but the way they dress nowadays . . ." He shrugged. "You could have laid her out in the casket in that dress when she first put it on."

Marti looked past the barricades, at girls who flirted and

4

boys who cajoled. Worst thing she could think of, burying a child.

"Does it look suspicious?"

"An arson investigator is checking it out. You can see the line of demarcation at the base of the stairs. Spread fast. Moved from the center of the building eastward. West end wasn't involved."

The front door was at the west end. "And that's where the bodies were found?"

"Right."

"Upstairs or down?"

"Downstairs was vacant."

They would have had to negotiate a flight of stairs. Maybe they could have gotten out.

"What kind of time frame have you got?"

"It was called in at 6:47. Almost half the building was involved when we got here four and a half minutes later."

"Be nice to know why the victims were in there and the doctor wasn't."

Ben grinned at her. "And I'm sure you'll find out."

Vik was in the alley, standing away from the building, talking to a tall, thin man who seemed to be ignoring him. They were almost the same height, but Vik was a bit taller at six two.

Vik had a tendency to lean over people. There was just a hint of ferocity in his face, with his beak nose bent from a break and his wiry eyebrows curling in all directions. There were dark pouches beneath his gray eyes that weren't caused by lack of sleep. Children would walk right up to him, but most adults found his appearance intimidating.

The other man glanced at Marti as she approached, then moved away.

"The doctor?" she asked Vik.

"Yeah. Edwards. James Edwards."

She watched him but didn't speak. In a few seconds he turned to her. "Yes?"

"Detective MacAlister." She showed him her shield.

"I certainly hope you don't want to ask questions, too. Not after this." He gestured toward the building.

He had the kind of voice she'd expect to hear if she were speaking with someone in broadcasting. Moderate tone. Perfect diction. No hint of where he came from. If she was listening to him without being able to see him, she would never guess that his skin was as smooth and as brown as the oak table in her kitchen.

"Good thing you weren't in there."

"Nobody should have been in there." He jammed his hands into his pockets. His slacks were tan, and clean.

"Why not?"

"Teresa called and said she'd be a few minutes late."

Marti waited. When he didn't volunteer anything else, she asked, "What time were you expecting her?"

"Seven, seven-fifteen."

Again she waited. "What time did you leave here today?"

As he looked at her, he seemed to be looking down his nose. He had a face she thought of as economical: narrow nose, thin lips, small, deep-set eyes. His ears stuck out a little, making him seem less stern and severe. Not talkative. At least not tonight. Shock, maybe. Perhaps grief, if he was fond of the receptionist, knew her well.

"How long did Teresa work for you?"

"Two years." He seemed almost mesmerized by the burned-out clinic.

"What time did you leave here today?" she asked again.

"Sixish."

"And when you got back?"

"The building was on fire."

"Did you call it in?" she asked.

"They were already here."

He had been away from the clinic for about fifty minutes. Not much time.

"Where did you go?"

"Is this some kind of interrogation?"

"I'm with Homicide. I have to know how the victims died, maybe why."

He took a few steps away from her. Without turning he said, "The electrical system and anything else in there that could possibly have caused this was upgraded before I moved in. I hadn't thought of that until now. How can I help you?"

"Anything unusual happen with the receptionist? Fight with the boyfriend?"

"I wouldn't know. I didn't see Teresa tonight, but she seemed fine on Tuesday. We had evening clinic two nights a week."

"What about the other victim?"

"Never saw her before. I have no idea why she was here. I can't even guess."

"And Teresa shouldn't have been here either?"

"Not that early."

"How did she get in?"

"She had a key."

"For the front or the back door?"

He seemed puzzled. "She had a key to both. I really should go to her mother. The poor woman's distraught."

Instead of leaving, he stood across from the back door and kept staring at the building.

2

Friday morning, after the autopsies, Marti and Vik walked the two blocks from the coroner's facility to the precinct. They worked in a two-story gray brick building in a municipal complex on the east side of town, not far from Lake Michigan.

"Probably the only time of day you can find a parking space around here," Vik said as they passed by the courthouse and the county building.

It was after seven.

"We've missed roll call and it's hot already," he complained. He wiped his forehead with a crumpled napkin that he seemed surprised to find in his pocket. "Great way to start the day. Be nice if Janet Petrosky didn't schedule these so early. Up half the night because of the fire, four hours' sleep when the alarm goes off . . ."

When Marti and Vik started working together, Marti had assumed he was surly because he didn't like having a female partner who was black as well. She knew now that it was nothing personal; Vik was grumpy most of the time. His attitude didn't bother her much because she wanted to work with someone who wouldn't get too friendly or ask too many questions about why she left a better-paying, higher-ranking position with the Chicago force to move here with her two kids and a dog. She didn't like talking about her husband, Johnny, whose death was the reason for the change.

Vik loosened his tie. "We've already had three, four kids

this year, dead because they were playing with matches. Now this. At least it was just the smoke that got to her."

Marti had drawn the short toothpick, making it her job to observe the unidentified victim's autopsy. "Mine never got off that table. Didn't try to run, nothing. Just laid there and died," Marti observed.

The girl was "high yellow," light-skinned, with delicate features and naturally straight hair. Pretty little thing. Small for her age. She had been dressed all in white, from the patent leather shoes to the lace attached to the barrette in her hair.

"Kid was two months pregnant and just a baby herself. Twelve years old, according to Doctor Cyprian. Doesn't fit any of the missing persons reports that have come across my desk in the past month or so."

Marti tried not to think of how thin the child was, or of the bruising and trauma that indicated recent physical and sexual abuse. She had been on the force in Chicago for ten years before moving sixty miles north to Lincoln Prairie, a little over a year ago. Many times she had attended more autopsies there in a week than she went to here in a month. She had seen many more dead children in Chicago, but it was easier to put them out of her mind then. Something about the frequency diminishing the effect, maybe. Here it was much harder to forget their faces and how they had died.

"The Martinez girl almost looked like she was sleeping," Vik said. "They'll be able to have an open casket."

"Nothing about a dead person looks like sleep to me. Dead is dead," Marti replied. Not knowing them used to make a difference, before Johnny died. Until then, losing someone you loved was what happened to somebody else. Johnny had been a Chicago cop, too. His death had changed her perception of every homicide she'd been involved with since. Maybe, if there were a little more action . . . "Sometimes things are too slow here."

"You want a few more fires, MacAlister? An arsonist from

the lunatic fringe? Another half dozen dead kids?" He kicked at a paper cup on the sidewalk.

A waist-high brick ledge surrounded this side of the county building. Petunias grew in lush profusion between the evergreen hedges planted there.

Vik snatched a fistful of hot pink blossoms. "Sounds like this Martinez girl was a nice kid," he said. "Mass and Communion every Sunday. Lived with her mother. Engaged to her older brother's friend. She was going to get married in December." He crushed the flowers and threw them on the sidewalk. "Want to walk over to the Barrister for breakfast?"

Eating was always the standard challenge after an autopsy.

"Swedish waffles?" he suggested.

The Puerto Rican cop Marti had worked with before she left the Chicago force always craved sushi after an autopsy. Vik always suggested something that required syrup. "I wonder if they serve brains and eggs," she said.

"Pig brains or cow brains?" Vik asked.

"I'm not sure. My father used to eat them. You scramble them together first, then fry them in butter." Her stomach lurched.

"What does it look like?"

"Kind of grayish when it's cooked. Might taste good with strawberry syrup."

When they reached the corner, Vik continued on to the precinct without even a glance down the street at the Barrister. This was the first time she'd been able to keep him from eating. She tried not to smile.

They spent the morning canvassing every home and business within a two-block radius of the clinic, and came up empty. Undaunted, they interviewed the Martinez girl's closest friends and Carmen Rodriguez, the girl who filled in at the clinic on evenings when Teresa couldn't work. The only things they could determine were that there had been no problems between Teresa and her boyfriend, and that she seemed very happy living at home with her mother and brother. Teresa's sisters broke into sobs in a matter of minutes.

"Damned waste of time," Vik complained.

"Teresa sounds like a candidate for sainthood."

"Beatification, at least," Vik agreed.

Marti didn't ask what that was.

When they got back to the precinct, they met with the lieutenant. "Dirty" Dan Dirkowitz had gained his nickname while playing linebacker for the Southern Illinois University Salukis. He was as large as the position required and still looked like an All-American: tall, blond, and muscle-bound. Marti liked him because he always assumed she was competent, and never commented on any distinctions between male and female officers the way her previous lieutenant in Chicago had.

The lieutenant's office was twice the size of the one Marti and Vik shared. He had a view of the easternmost part of the city and a glimpse of Lake Michigan. The football he kept on his desk was turned so that she could see the autograph when she sat down: Mike Ditka. The only other thing of interest on the desk was a defused hand grenade. Dan's oldest brother had died in Vietnam. Johnny had served there too.

"What have you got?" Dirkowitz asked.

"Nothing," Vik said. "No suspects, no motive. If Arson steps it up a bit we might get their report within the next six months. That might tell us something."

"Monday morning," Dirkowitz promised. "Except for any lab analysis—that takes longer." Just over thirty, he looked even younger as he ran his fingers through precisely clipped blond hair. "I need an expeditious arrest on this one."

Expeditious arrest meant that since the dead receptionist was Hispanic and the unidentified victim black, community leaders representing both minorities were making noises. Marti hated that kind of pressure, especially if the newspaper got involved.

"How loud are they yelling?" she asked.

"Nobody's hostile yet."

She relaxed.

"I wonder if Vern Halloran and his pro-life group are behind it," Vik said. "The doctor who owns the place does abortions at Lincoln Prairie General. They've been passing out literature at that clinic since the middle of May."

"We were going to interview Reverend Halloran this afternoon," Marti said, "but he's joined that protest over the resumption of abortions at Cook County Hospital. One of the photographs we got last night shows part of the front fender of a white subcompact. Halloran owns a white Escort that's been observed near the clinic by officers monitoring the pamphlet giveaways. We haven't been able to get a make on the vehicle in the photo."

The lieutenant toyed with the hand grenade. "This is where they live. I don't think Halloran wants that kind of publicity here. Thanks to someone on their deacon's board, the *News-Times* ignored the business with the pamphlets and looked the other way when they were picketing the hospital. I've heard rumors that they stopped the picketing because hospital management is going to change the abortion policy."

"The real question," Marti said, "is why they singled out Doctor Edwards. He's not the only doctor here who does abortions."

"Another possible suspect is Edwards himself," Vik said. "Even though doctors seem to be richer than Rockefeller, a lot of times when these businesses go up, the owner's done it, or paid to have it done."

"What about the anonymous tip we got from the hotline?" Dirkowitz asked. "Good PR if that one proves out."

"R.D.?" Vik scoffed.

"Reginald Davies," the lieutenant confirmed. "Pimp, dope pusher." He pulled the pin on the grenade. "Garbage that I don't want here."

"We gave that one to Vice," Vik said. "Let him deal with someone he's familiar with."

"Low profile," Marti added. "I'd rather not have him think we're seriously considering him a suspect until we get something solid. He lives in Chicago most of the time, even though he still owns that house over on Greenview."

"And we do have an unidentified minor." The lieutenant dropped the grenade on his desk blotter, signaling the end of the meeting. "Keep me apprised. The minor concerns me. I don't like what I see in the coroner's preliminary report. We're midway between Chicago and Milwaukee. God knows how many kids pass through here heading north. And there's a whole hell of a lot of trouble they can get themselves into. I don't want that kind of trouble happening here."

On the elevator, Marti turned to Vik. "I'm going to tour that clinic before we get the Arson report."

He glared at her. She could almost hear what he was thinking: intuition. "Men's work, policing," he had said her first day on the job. "We're professionals here. We do not carry illegal weapons. We do not draw our weapons on the least pretext. We reason. We remain calm and detached. We investigate. We don't let anything as unreliable as intuition interfere with common sense and sound judgment."

He seemed a little perturbed now as she laughed. Then he muttered, "Big city cop" just loud enough for her to hear it. But she wasn't, not anymore.

3

After roll call Saturday morning, Marti drove over to the burned-out clinic. Vik came along. There had been no break in the heat, and neither of them had had much sleep the past two nights. After their meeting with the lieutenant yesterday they each had visited five members of the Reverend Mr. Halloran's pro-life group. Without exception, the members were convinced that by picketing the clinic they were doing the work of the Lord. Nobody could come up with any reason for singling out that particular clinic, except that the clientele was poor, and the poor were easily led, and exploited. Marti didn't agree with their logic. She didn't even understand it.

As she pulled up in front of the clinic she saw that Ben Walker was waiting for them. She wondered if he'd volunteered to show them around or had been delegated. She had been able to avoid discussing anything personal with him on the night of the fire, but that could be more difficult today. Ben wanted to take the boys on a camping trip, week after next. She wasn't sure she wanted Theo to go.

The clinic had been boarded up and covered with dangerous-structure warnings. A bitter, acrid smell filled the air.

Ben ambled over. "We'll have to go in through the side door." He led the way. "Inspector says it's safe enough for a quick look-see."

In the dark, confined space, the smoky odor permeated the water-drenched walls, ceiling, and floor. Every surface was covered with a sticky layer of damp soot. Water dripped somewhere in loud, measured drops. Marti felt the floor, warped in places, give a little beneath her weight. It made her uneasy.

Ben saw her looking down. "Subbasement," he said. "Floor's sound." He turned on his flashlight, creating a spotlight effect. "You can see the line of demarcation in the area surrounding the stairs."

There was a gaping space where the stairwell had been, and a metal railing dangled from the second floor.

"Alcohol was used as an accelerant, and the pour pattern extends from the stairs to three feet from the back door. The heaviest concentration is at the base of the stairs," Ben explained. He seemed so at ease, as if the waterlogged ceiling couldn't fall on them or the floor give way at any time. "The fire started near the door and spread to the upstairs. It moved eastward, leaving the west side undamaged, except for smoke and water. The arsonist would have had to stand well away from the point of ignition. The flash point was too high. Must have stood near the door and tossed in a lit packet of matches. He closed the door. That gave him time to get away before the fire was observed by someone outside. And the arsonist was smart enough not to set himself on fire."

"How long did the fire burn before you got here?" Marti asked.

"You'll have to wait for the report. Unofficially, about twenty minutes."

Marti turned to Vik. "The doctor said he left about six. The fire started about thirty minutes later. Edwards returned at approximately six-fifty. He had expected the Martinez girl to arrive later than usual, between seven and seven-fifteen. I'd guess that ordinarily, Teresa Martinez would have arrived about the time he returned."

"Just the kind of case I like," Vik said. "Uncomplicated. We either have someone who didn't know the schedule, someone who did and just wanted to burn the place down, someone who arranged to have the little girl here so he could kill her and make it seem accidental. . . ."

"I know," she agreed. "A cast of thousands. We wouldn't want this case to get boring."

"The way the fire was set, if anyone had opened the upstairs door at the wrong time, the oxygen up there would have brought the fire right to them," Ben said.

"So we've either got a clever perp or a lucky one," Vik said.

"I can't narrow that one down for you. We've got three suspicious-origin fires right now, and we're satisfied that we're looking for three different arsonists. No firebug in town." Ben swung the flashlight in a wide arc. "For the most part we get the simple mom-and-pop stuff, setting fire to the failing business, or we get the revenge-type fires. This fire was not set in an area that we can say was intended to cause the destruction of the doctor's records, or his equipment. That's the most typical indication that the owner had the fire set, even though it's impossible to predict what fire will do once it gets going."

He swung the flashlight to the back door. It had a deadbolt lock that required a key on both sides. Marti tested the floor, hesitated when it creaked, then went to look for signs of forced entry. There were none. Teresa had had keys to the front and back doors. Could she have left the back door open?

"And," Ben said, "this is also unofficial: all locks were changed two weeks ago because a set of keys was lost. The key in the Martinez girl's purse marked 'front door' did not fit the lock. That'll be in the report."

So even if Teresa had made it down the stairs, she wouldn't have been able to get out.

"Thanks," Marti said.

"According to the doctor, the closet where the alcohol was stored is over here," Ben said. He went to the wall not far from where the fire had started. At each step, the floor groaned and yielded.

Marti had to stand close to Ben to get a look inside the

supply closet. She noticed that he had shaved before coming over. As she peered into the closet, she inhaled a whiff of lime.

"Looks like janitor's supplies," Ben said. The broom had plastic bristles that hadn't melted from the heat. There was a thick, heavy mop in a bucket. A foxtail hung on a hook beside a dustpan. Water had saturated rolls of toilet paper, and there was the sour smell of wet cleaning rags. "I can't take you upstairs, but there's another closet above this one."

He outlined the floor plan, pointing upward as he indicated where each girl was found. "There was also a room used as a storage area. The doctor told the investigator that he used it to store some surgical equipment he brought with him when he moved from Chicago. Said he had thought he might be able to sell it, but that he didn't have the time to look into it."

"Do you know much about him?" Marti asked.

"Not really. This is the only women's clinic in the area since they closed one about six blocks from here a couple of years ago. That place was comprehensive, had a pediatric clinic too."

"And now there's nothing," Vik said. "Damned shame." He took a step back. Wood cracked. "For cryin'—" His foot sank and he froze, not daring to move.

"Jessenovik," Marti said. "Don't tell me you've got your foot caught. Talk about an accident waiting to happen."

Ben went to him, testing the floor with each step, stopping a short distance away. "Try lifting your foot out."

"Stuck," Vik muttered.

"Try to get your foot out of your shoe."

Marti watched anxiously as Vik crouched, then reached into the hole, fumbling around. In a few minutes he had freed his foot but not his shoe. "Damn." He took his time reaching the door, awkward with only one shoe on.

When he reached the safety of the doorway, he said, "The smoke alarms—the News-Times said they worked. Did they?"

"They were operational," Ben said. "The girl just panicked. She could have run down the front stairs."

"With a key that wouldn't open the door," Marti reminded them. She took one more look around. She felt angry. Maybe it was the smell or the extent of the damage. Maybe it was the thought of a panic-stricken young woman who hadn't found a way out. She walked carefully to the door, avoiding the area where Vik's foot had gone through the floor.

Ben knelt and rummaged around beneath the floorboard. It took him less than a minute to free Vik's shoe. "Need to wipe it off on something," he said, handing it to Marti.

"Thanks," she said, blinking in the bright sunlight as they walked outside. She started to say "I owe you one," but hesitated when she remembered the camping trip.

"Both of the trucks are at a fire," Ben said. "I was going off duty so I was free to come over here." He smiled, a wide grin that crinkled the corners of his eyes. She could like him a lot if she wanted to.

Marti stopped at Vik's house so he could change his socks. When they got back to the precinct, she changed into a blouse she had brought from home. There was only a faint odor of smoke clinging to her clothing, but she didn't need the reminder.

She and Vik shared a corner office on the second floor with two Vice cops. Although the room was crowded with four desks, it seemed airy and spacious after the windowless room where she had worked in Chicago. Windows the length of two walls provided a view of the courthouse and the new jail across the street. When she took time to notice, she could glimpse the tops of a cluster of trees a block away. A limp, brown spider plant that someone had abandoned on the windowsill one night was thriving now on a diet of cold coffee and warm pop.

The Vice cops, Slim and Cowboy, had decorated the walls before Marti joined the group. Posters and pinups were not allowed, but calendars were. One, turned to December, featured a nearly nude model cradling a two-way radio between pendulous breasts. Another calendar turned to February showed a busty brunette looking lustily at a Smith & Wesson. The only calendar turned to the current month was a small one on her desk that her son Theo had affixed to Popsicle sticks. Unlike the drawers, the top of her desk was tidy: the calendar; a snapshot of her with Johnny, Theo, and Joanna taken four months before Johnny died; a bright blue ceramic mug that Joanna had made; and a pencil holder from Theo—more Popsicle sticks glued on a juice can with a decoupaged picture of Bigfoot, their dog.

Marti and Vik hadn't been in the office five minutes when they heard thick-soled boots clumping into the room, followed by the intense odor of Obsession for Men. Without looking up from the report she was writing, Marti said, "Hope you've got something new and exciting to tell us about Reginald Davies, Cowboy. You too, Slim."

Cowboy ambled over to Vik's desk. "You two relics ain't got any leads in this arson case yet, huh?" he drawled.

Slim put a box of doughnuts by the coffeepot and selected a jelly-filled. "Relics, hell. Vik might be older than Lake Michigan, but Marti here ain't old worth a damn." His fingertips brushed her hair.

She glanced up at him, saw the cupid's-bow smile that gave an innocent sweetness to his just-darker-than-tan face. She had never worked Vice, never wanted to, couldn't think of too many Vice cops who weren't cynics and also flirts.

She coughed, pretending to choke on the heavy scent of Obsession, and waved her arm. "Fine line between smelling good and stinking, Slim. You're leaning heavily to stink this morning."

Slim kept smiling. "You noticed."

"What did you find out about R.D.?"

"Man's got an alibi," Cowboy said. "Man's got such a damned good alibi it makes me wonder why he needs one."

"He was here, at Esperanza's," Slim said. "That Mexican restaurant on Webster near Jefferson."

"And," Cowboy added, "he was eating tamales and drinking sangria for three hours. Whole damned time that clinic was burning down and an hour before and an hour after."

"Sounds like the man wanted an alibi," Slim agreed. "Got seven people giving him one, too. We thought we ran the man out of town, except for visitin'. Looks like we need to lock him up."

"You haven't been able to yet," Vik complained. "And you had enough chances."

"What can I say?" Slim said. "Man's slick."

"He commands a lot of loyalty," Cowboy said. "Not just one or two people lying for him. Six or seven. We did make it hard enough for him to run his hookers and his drugs here that he took his operation to Chicago."

"Where it had damned well better stay." Slim smiled at Marti again and took another doughnut.

"I've got a dead minor," she reminded them. "You think he could be involved?"

"Minors are the main reason we harassed him," Cowboy told her. "I believe he just about raised those two little ladies he brings with him when he comes here."

"One of them, Linda, was born here," Slim said. "She's the one who sprays those party colors in her hair. Other one's named Glodine."

Marti had seen Linda before. She didn't dye her hair—too permanent, maybe. Instead, it was always streaked with bright colors, red, yellow, blue, so that the natural black showed through. She matched her clothes to her hair or vice versa.

"How long has Linda been with him?" Marti asked.

"We think since she was twelve," Slim said. "She was a real hellion, in trouble since grade school. Time she was eleven she was running a shoplifting ring and she was the youngest member. Supposedly her mother sent her to live with relatives, but that's just about the time R.D. split for Chicago. My bet's that she went with him."

"So, he does like them young," she said.

"Apparently so. He married a local girl he put on the block and she left here time their two girls were eight, ten years old. Rumor has it R.D.'s mother helped her get away from him. The wife had been with him since she was about thirteen, so she could have had a good reason for leaving—protecting her own kids. We never could pin anything on R.D. He hangs out with this guy named Brick. Enforcer, bodyguard, whatever. Brick was a wrestler at Illinois State. And a pre-law major. When we did bring R.D. in, he was so well primed by Brick, or somebody, that he thought he was too slick to need a lawyer."

"So," Cowboy grinned. "We just harassed him until he left town."

"What if he's back for a while?" Marti asked.

"Won't be here for long," Cowboy promised.

"Won't be here at all if he's bringing minors to town," Slim agreed.

She believed them.

4

After lunch, Marti decided to see if the Reverend Mr. Halloran was at home. Vik almost smiled as they got into their unmarked car.

"My father and his were friends," he said.

"Vik! You must know at least one member of half the families in Lincoln Prairie. Ninety thousand isn't exactly a small town."

"It used to be. There was one high school then, just like they're going back to now. You got to know a lot of people, and most of them, and their kids, and their grandkids are still here. You knew who was related to the aldermen and the mayor, and whose dad was a good plumber or electrician, where to buy used cars, which families owned local businesses. Halloran's dad was a minister, very active in the community. My dad and my uncles were involved in a lot of things, too."

Marti smiled and shook her head. "Takes getting used to." She had realized how different it was here when her neighbor was featured in the *News-Times* for winning the local vegetable garden contest. The local newspaper read like a gossip sheet sometimes, reporting divorces, births, and traffic violations.

Halloran lived on the northwest side of town, not far from the golf course. It was a secluded neighborhood, and the tree-lined street Marti turned onto was just wide enough for two lanes of traffic.

"When's Theo going on that camping trip?" Vik asked. "Next weekend, isn't it?"

"Week after. Maybe."

Vik consulted his notes. "You own a white, 1989 Ford Escort?"

"My wife's car, yes."

Someone could have seen the car the police photos only glimpsed. They had only the fender in one photo.

"Where was that car the night of the fire?" Vik asked.

"I've been through this with the other officers."

"This is in connection with a homicide investigation, not arson," Vik reminded him.

"This is an excuse to harass me because of my pro-life activism."

"Sir, we don't care what activities you're involved in as long as you don't break the law. Where was the car the night of the fire?"

"In the garage."

"Thank you."

"Is that all?"

"For now."

"I'm going to talk with someone about this continued questioning," Halloran said. "Someone has to defend the rights of the unborn."

"Those two young girls who died had a right to life, too," Vik said.

Marti was the last to leave the room, walking behind the reverend and Vik as they went down the hall. They passed two other rooms before they got to the front door. The first one was dark, curtains drawn. A teenage girl was standing inside, holding a feather duster and looking as if she'd been eavesdropping. The girl must be the reverend's daughter. Marti tried to remember her name. She was on the high school swim team and had pestered Joanna the entire school year to join the Athletes for Jesus.

Wendy, she remembered as they got to the front door. Outside, the sun was almost blinding.

CHAPTER 5

Danny Jones crossed the unlit parking lot and stopped at the gravel shoulder, which dropped abruptly to a narrow stream about three stories below street level. Thick weeds and bushes brushed against his face as he hunched down near the concrete abutments where the street spanned the ravine. Not that anyone was likely to see him waiting here. No traffic and no people around this time of night. Not too many more during the day.

He wiped sweat from his forehead. Heat, but mostly nerves. He just wanted to get out of here. Get away from this place. Virgie would be here in a few more minutes, and then they could leave. Go home.

But home to what? Everything got put in the street while he was in jail and they lost everything. At least he knew a few things now that he didn't know before he got locked up. Like, maybe Social Security for Virgie. He'd look into that once he got back. He wasn't found guilty of nothing. He ought to be able to get work.

He leaned back on his heels, picked up a stone, threw it down to the water. Heard something—a rat, probably. He'd have to find a place to stay back home. Real quick. They'd have to stay in a shelter for a few days. Be hard on Virgie, but it wouldn't be for long.

The car's engine seemed loud in the stillness. He stood up, walked toward it. The headlights were out. He couldn't see Virgie. As he ran toward the car, it picked up speed and rushed at him.

6

When Marti arrived at the parking lot, four patrol cars were parked along its perimeter. There was one abandoned house at the north edge of the lot, a secondhand store to the south. Sherman Avenue was east of the area and Garden Street was to the west, spanning the ravine where the body had been found. Marti wiped her brow. Still humid. She had gone off duty a little after nine, and thirty minutes later got a call at home. Vik hadn't arrived yet.

It was Thursday, a week to the day since the fire at Lakeshore Clinic. That had drawn a larger crowd. She pulled up behind a squad car and watched as half a dozen teenagers jostled each other, laughing and talking above the rap music that spewed from a tape player. Several young children tried to push past a cluster of adults who blocked their view. She scanned their faces, didn't see anyone she recognized. Reaching for her camera case, she got out of the car.

She shouldered her way through the crowd without identifying herself. Lupe Torres came toward her, a petite uniformed officer with thirty pounds of equipment resting on her broad hips. "The victim is a black male, fell about halfway down the ravine. A couple of teenagers were walking across the bridge and happened to look down. Burdette's keeping folks away from the bridge. Nobody's set foot in the parking lot or been near any access point to the ravine since we got here."

Lupe had been on the force for two years. If Marti could have requested the first officer on the scene, Lupe would have been the one. "How'd you get stuck with a showboat like Burdette?" she asked, glancing at the tall, blond rookie.

"Oh, he's improving." There was an edge to Lupe's voice that implied she wouldn't tolerate less.

Marti smiled.

"And Isaac the Wino is sleeping one off way over by the Dumpster near that house. Says he didn't see nothing, same as always. I left him there so he'd be available for questioning."

"See any familiar faces in the crowd?"

"Few locals I know. Nobody we could put a make on."

"Request a narc and a gang specialist to scan the bystanders, and tell the evidence techs to set up some lights along the edge of the parking lot. Then wait while I talk with Isaac. You're taking notes?"

"Yes ma'am."

"Good. Continue recording on this one."

As Marti approached the Dumpster she heard Isaac snoring. Just her luck that he might be her only witness. Isaac "never saw nothin'," as he put it. He might admit to hearing something if the question were properly phrased, but he would never acknowledge seeing anything.

She gave the lid of the open Dumpster a push with her flashlight and let it bang shut. Isaac jumped but didn't wake up.

She squatted, turning her face upwind to avoid the odor of dirty clothes and sweat and his alcohol-saturated breath.

"Hey, Isaac." She shook him awake. "What do you know about this?"

"Huh?" He woke up all at once, eyes bleary and bloodshot but fully alert. "Hey. Huh? Oh. Officer Mac." His speech was slow but not slurred. "Isaac ain't seen nothin'. Swear to God."

"What did you hear?"

Isaac's current residence was the nearby house. He had sat on the sagging steps just last month and watched someone get robbed and beaten up without "seeing nothin'." He did hear one mugger call the other by name, though, and it only took Marti two trips back to see him to extract that information. She knew he did this because he liked the company, so she tried to spend a few extra minutes with him, just talking.

Isaac shifted, sitting up straighter. "Coulda heard somethin', now. Jes' coulda." He groped behind his back and pulled out a bottle of Mad Dog 20-20. "Ah." He held the bottle up to the light, then shook it near his ear. "Empty. Damn."

He held on to the bottle. "Jes' settin' here restin' my eyes. Sometimes they goes to burnin' like and I gotta close 'em so's not to go blind. Coulda heard a thump like, and some glass breakin' and a kind of scrapin' sound, like this."

He made a noise that set her teeth on edge. "Car ease along kinda slow, speed up all at once. *Scree!* Car back up. *Scree!* Woman say, 'Son of a bitch!' Door slam. Car drive off. Burnin' rubber. I ain't seen nothin', though. Isaac ain't seen nothin'." He checked the bottle again, seemed disappointed that no wine had materialized, stashed it behind his back. He had said as much as he wanted.

"Recognize the voice?"

"How I s'posed to know who's talkin' if'n that's all they say?" He was getting irritable. "Didn't sound like nobody I know." Arms folded, he leaned back and closed his eyes.

No use pushing him when he was through talking, or he wouldn't say anything more later. "I'll be stopping by later, Isaac. Just in case you remember something else you heard. Or recognize the voice."

She walked back to the evidence techs and told the print man to check for tire marks first, then proceed with the usual routine. Yellow scene-of-crime tape marked off the entire area. More uniforms, several detectives, and an ambulance had arrived. Dr. Cyprian, the medical examiner, was on his way.

Marti then spoke with the two teenagers who had found the body.

"Threw a pop can down there," the taller of the two told her. "Thought it was just some old clothes at first."

"It was the way it was shaped made us look again," the other one said. "Shaped like a body. We saw the cops parked up by Jefferson. Went and told them."

"Some old drunk," the tall kid said. "Got too close to the edge and fell."

"Anyone else around?" Marti asked.

"Nah. Nobody much comes around here at night. We was just going over to a friend's. See, ain't even no traffic."

Vik pulled up at the curb. He slammed the door as he got out of his car, then scowled at a moon-faced little boy peering over the hood as he walked by the uniform standing at the entrance to the parking lot.

Marti put a telephoto lens on her camera and snapped half a dozen pictures. Vik began whistling something tuneless and irritating. He still thought she was playing big-city cop when she used the camera. All she wanted was her own record of what she saw at the crime scene.

They each had their own routine. Vik talked with Lupe, checking her notes. Marti kept out of the evidence techs' way, going into an area only when they indicated it was okay. Collecting evidence was a tedious process, and it took Marti more than an hour to reach the gravel near the ravine. She photographed the skid marks that swung toward the abrupt drop to the bottom, and the deeper ruts made by a car put into reverse. One tech said there were stall marks, that the car had reversed, stopped, started moving again.

After Cyprian arrived and examined the victim with his usual thoroughness, Marti and Vik went down. She had a hard time keeping her balance, but kept snapping photographs as she approached. The man's face, scored with abrasions, was twisted toward her at a strange angle. One eye was partially out of the socket. His torn T-shirt exposed jagged cuts on his torso, some deep enough to expose a whitish layer of fatty tissue. A piece of green glass protruded from his side. His jeans were torn at the knees, old tears, not caused by being hit and dragged. Soiled at the crotch, smelly. Must have let go of everything when he was hit.

Ignoring the odor, Marti pulled on a pair of thin latex gloves, squatted beside the dead man, and touched his face, his shoulder, one arm. Still cooling, no rigor yet. Pebbles were embedded in his skin, and his thin, bony arms were bruised.

She hardly noticed the blood. She had gotten used to that years ago. But just for a moment, she wanted to ease him into a more natural position, as if it would make him more comfortable. "His spirit's walkin'," Momma would say, because his killer was unknown.

When the odor of human excreta became intrusive, she scrabbled up the side of the ravine and paused at the top to make notes. It was almost midnight and most of the onlookers were gone. She and Vik would have to canvass the neighborhood first thing tomorrow.

Vik, who still considered interviewing women's work, was consulting with the evidence techs.

"Yeah, right, sure," the tech grumbled. "Like I ain't never done this before. Better make sure I didn't use the stiff's toes to get fingerprints." The tech snapped his notebook shut and walked away.

"I never paid much attention to this area," Marti said. "Interesting."

"Yeah," Vik agreed. "That ravine's been here since the glacier retreated. Twelve thousand years and they haven't bulldozed it yet."

Lupe came up to them. "Got another one for you," she said. "Five-seventeen Jericho. Female, caucasian, old. Identified as a Ruth Price."

C H A P T E R

7

About fifteen minutes later Marti stood in a basement kitchenette-apartment looking down at Ruth Price's body. The dim circle of light from a small lamp with an age-stained fringed shade was supplemented by two bright-beamed flashlights held by uniforms.

Marti squatted beside the elderly woman. Ruth Price was lying facedown, her pale forehead on an old flatiron against the wall. It looked as if the woman had fallen on it, but Marti knew there was too much blood and tissue for it to have been a fall.

She looked at the old woman's hands, mottled with liver spots. Knuckles swollen, probably from joint disease. She looked at the soft gray hair, trimmed short. Ruth Price was seventy at least, she decided. Maybe she had been surprised and died without having time to feel pain or fear. But there was always something wrong about someone living this long only to die a violent death.

An evidence tech came up behind Marti. When he cleared his throat she got up and moved out of his way. "I came in this way." She indicated the straight path from the door to the body. "Same as the neighbor upstairs who found her. You might find a few of the neighbor's prints. Told the uniform she's not sure what she touched, just that she came in, went to the body, and backed out."

She took a flashlight out of her purse and made slow, swinging arcs. Two small windows higher than the top of her head opened in from the side of the house. The frames were rotting. One window was secured with a hook lock and slide bolt. The other had been pushed open and was still ajar. It hadn't required much pressure for someone to push the screws from the frame. Looking out, she could see tall grass and weeds.

She scanned the room. A full-sized metal-frame bed covered with a dingy white sheet took up most of the space. The white enamel sink had a rust stain in the basin and a steady stream of water trickling from the faucet. A bowl, cup, and spoon had been washed and left on a dish towel on the drainboard. She looked into the paper bag that served as a wastebasket. One empty can, chicken noodle soup. A peach stone. An orange rind.

When she got the nod from the techs, Marti investigated but failed to find evidence that anything had been stolen. The television was a small black-and-white, and the radio was an old wooden one with tubes inside. Probably didn't even work anymore. She didn't turn it on. There was a Kodak Brownie Hawkeye on a shelf in the closet. She doubted you could still buy film for a camera like that.

Nothing here worth stealing. It was the last Thursday in July, too early for Social Security checks and too late for anyone living on them to have much money.

Marti nodded to Vik, who was following a technician around and taking notes, and headed upstairs to see the neighbor who had found the body.

Mrs. Banks was a tiny, dark-skinned woman with sunken cheeks and no teeth. She wouldn't take the chain off the door to let Marti into her apartment, but she was willing to talk to her. "Balm in Gilead" was playing somewhere inside, and Marti could smell something simmered with smoked meat.

"Hard to believe somebody got poor old Ruthie," the old woman said. "Lord have mercy. Ain't nair' one of us safe in our own beds anymore. Good woman, Ruthie. Took care of old Price right up 'til he died. And him bedridden, too."

The old woman's eyes were puffy and red. Her voice trembled as she spoke. "Ain't right, jus' ain't right."

"She live here long?" Marti asked.

"Musta been here since maybe nineteen-fifty, 'fifty-five. I moved in right about the time they killed John Kennedy, and they'd been here a long while then. Used to be right next door here. Ruthie had to move downstairs after old Price died, couldn't afford the upstairs rent no more." Mrs. Banks shook her head. Her hair was so thin Marti could see her scalp.

"What made you go downstairs tonight?"

"Got to be ten past ten and Ruthie wasn't here to watch the news with me. Did that every night. I knowed something musta been wrong. Not expectin' nothin' like that, though. Got two locks myself and this here chain."

"You need a dead bolt, ma'am," Marti explained. "You call Bethel Baptist and they'll send someone around to install one for you. No charge."

Mrs. Banks looked at her as if she didn't believe in something for nothing anymore. "Ain't got no phone."

"It's part of a program for senior citizens, ma'am. I can give them a call if you'd like."

Still looking skeptical, Mrs. Banks considered the offer. "Well, since it's the church, I suppose it's all right. But they will have identification on them, won't they?"

"Yes, ma'am. Did you see Ruth Price at all today?"

Mrs. Banks hitched up her slip. "Thursday, ain't it. Ruthie went to Truman Park. Did that most every Thursday the weather was good."

The old woman was beginning to enjoy having someone to talk to. Marti didn't try to hurry her along.

"Old Price used to work downtown someplace. Got paid on Thursday and Ruthie'd meet him at lunchtime and they'd have themselves a little picnic in the park." Mrs. Banks began making chewing motions even though she didn't have anything in her mouth.

"Would she have carried anything valuable in her purse?" Someone could have set her up as a mark.

"Ruthie ain't had nothin' what was valuable."

"Money?"

Mrs. Banks shook her head. "Young 'uns see a coupla dollars, knock you over the head gettin' to it."

"Would she talk to someone she didn't know?"

"Little children maybe. Never had none of her own. Wouldn't hardly talk to no one else though, exceptin' me."

Marti thought about the window used to gain access. "See anyone around here today, 'round by the side of the house maybe?"

"Thought I heard somethin' out there yestidday. Figured it was kids playin' around. Yelled out the window at 'em. Funny, though. Kids or an animal woulda taken off. Whatever this was, noise just stopped."

Marti made a note to check the side of the house and have the evidence techs take a look.

"Oh," Mrs. Banks said. "That Avon lady what came through here couple days ago. Wouldn't think nothin' of it, but long as I been livin' here, she's the first. And rude, too. Tellin' me I gotta open this door. Nothin' like them Avon ladies you used to see on TV."

"What did she look like?"

"Oh, I didn't open my door. Chile didn't sound old enough to tell me what to do. Ruthie saw her, though. Said she didn't have nair' sample and looked about like she sounded, skirt up to her behind and a pound of makeup on her face. Course most all of these young girls dress that way nowadays. And Ruthie told me to be careful. Thought the girl might be casin' the place. Said she didn't have nothin' for nobody to steal." Her voice broke.

"Did Mrs. Price have any family?"

"Niece." She wiped her eyes. "Lives in St. Louis. Never came here so I never met her, but she sent hankies and perfume at Christmas. I'll get her address for you. Ruthie and me give each other our next of kin, just in case."

Mrs. Banks left the chain on and the door ajar while she went to get the information. Marti thought about Truman Park, a corner lot of wooded land with green metal turtles to climb on. The place didn't attract teenagers and was located in a conspicuous, well-trafficked area. If this case wasn't resolved by next Thursday, she might take a walk over there. It was the kind of thing she'd never had time for on the force in Chicago.

8

By the time Marti left the house where Ruth Price had lived, the old woman's body had been removed. The street was deserted and the neighborhood quiet. She checked her slacks. Lots of snags. Ruined. It had been too hot for the matching jacket. The temperature had hit ninety-seven today. It was cooler now, but not by much. A cricket chorus chirped in the knee-high grass that surrounded the house, and she could smell stagnant water nearby.

She slapped at a mosquito, then flicked on her flashlight and walked to the side of the building. A concrete path led to the windows that opened into Ruth Price's flat. When she touched the window that had been forced, it swung in. The hinges were rusty but didn't squeak. She touched the corroded metal. The hinges had been oiled. The tech hadn't found any prints. Someone had waited here, perhaps observing Ruth Price while she was inside, and entered without being heard.

Ruth Price had not been raped. She didn't have money or valuables, and every thief in town would know that any assistance check she might receive wasn't due for another week. An old woman, helpless against violence, had been selected as a victim and killed. The muscles in Marti's jaw tightened. Premeditated murders angered her more than impulse killings.

She wiped the traces of oil from her fingertips. No motive. No suspect. This was the type of case she often had been forced to file when she worked in Chicago. Here, at least she would have more time to investigate.

Vik was still inside, probably worrying the evidence techs.

She returned to the front of the house to wait for him. The porch steps creaked under her weight. It was an old house, sandwiched between a smaller unoccupied wood frame and a bungalow. White paint was peeling and the screen door hung by one hinge.

A light went on in the bungalow and a pregnant woman in silhouette walked past the window. Nobody had been home there when Marti arrived at the scene. Now a battered green Pinto was parked out front. Someone began picking out chords on a guitar then strummed a few bars of a song. A child laughed and the music stopped.

Ignoring the dirt on the top step, she sat down. This neighborhood on the south side of Lincoln Prairie had once been middle-class. Over the years, the original owners had "bought up" and moved to other communities—towns like Gurnee, Mundelein, Lindenhurst. Many of the new residents took an equal pride in ownership and maintained their homes and property. Even so, this area, which began six blocks west of Lake Michigan, had become pockmarked with neglected buildings in need of repair. Some of the larger houses, like this one, were sectioned into as many small apartments as the plumbing, heating, and electrical systems could support. Drug and gang activity in this part of town had increased.

Marti had not expected the ethnic diversity that she found in Lincoln Prairie. Swedes, Finns, Germans, Hispanics, Filipinos, West Indians, and African Americans coexisted with little overt friction. A nearby church celebrated occasional Croatian or Serbian masses as well as a mass in Spanish each Sunday. She liked living in a place where her kids could go to public schools that represented so many cultures.

In Chicago they had attended a predominantly black private school where drugs and gangs weren't part of the curriculum. Now that the two high schools were going to merge, she was concerned about the impact of three thousand students at one facility. She was worried, too, about the increase in drug and gang activity here. But overall, the move out of Chicago was a good one for her children, even if the real reason she came here was to have a quiet place to brood over Johnny's death.

Four years ago Johnny had volunteered for a special narcotics unit. He didn't discuss his assignments with her, and she didn't ask for any explanation of the long hours he put in. It was almost two years since he died. It didn't seem that long since first her captain, then the coroner, told her that Johnny had put the muzzle of his gun in his mouth and pulled the trigger. She still didn't believe them. Next week she would visit his grave. He would have been forty years old August 2.

Marti was angry with the entire Chicago force. Because they hadn't protected him. Because they believed he was a suicide. So she came here, to the one friend she had known since childhood, to a small city with a small force and, she thought, little crime. She had expected to work uneventful eight-hour shifts and have plenty of time to grieve. Because she liked being a cop, she also had hoped the work wouldn't be too boring.

Once here, she found out that the crime rate was lower than Chicago's, her case load much lighter, but she still dealt with the same types of crime. Children were abused, drugs were sold, tricks were turned, and the bunko scams were old and unimaginative. Young men were run down by cars, too, but until tonight she hadn't known of any who had been flung into a ravine. And old women got their heads bashed in, but not often.

The only meaningful difference from the job in Chicago was having enough time to get the job done, to follow through and follow up and accomplish something by the end of most days. She didn't feel as overworked, didn't get as frustrated, and often felt as if she had done something good, like getting help for a teenage offender instead of watching him get caught up in the system and become a lifelong criminal.

Nearby, someone gunned an engine and tires squealed. Marti could hear Vik inside, asking an evidence tech if he'd dusted for prints under the rim of the bathroom sink.

She smiled. Arrogant SOB, she had thought. Vik's attitude,

that policing was "men's work," wasn't out of line with unofficial departmental policy. There were special rules for her: Be twice as good, twice as smart, and work twice as hard. She was no longer certain whether those rules existed because she was black, or because she was female. She accepted it because nobody would understand what she was talking about if she complained. She had never cared about wearing a uniform or carrying a shield and a weapon, but valued the authority they represented. She hoped she wouldn't abuse what power she had, but she refused to be excluded from the exercise of power.

The male officers she worked with soon forgot or overlooked the black, female distinctions, just as Vik was learning to do. In a life-threatening situation, street smarts, decisiveness, a clear head, and steady aim were more important. Those situations occurred frequently in Chicago, but she seldom had to draw her weapon here.

Behind her, the door slammed. It was Vik. "Through in there, Jessenovik?" Marti asked. "Took you long enough to tell the evidence techs their job."

"I wrote up an inventory and checked it out with that Mrs. Banks upstairs. She was real sure nothing's missing."

"Whoever did this took the time to oil the hinges on the window before going in."

Vik shoved his hands in his pockets. "It's a real pain in the butt when they decide to think things through first. Give me a good, solid, random victim. A senseless, stupid crime. Much easier to catch the knuckleheads when they don't try to be clever."

"Makes you wonder. Why would someone set her up?"

"Now look, Marti, don't make too much of it. It was probably just some kid who watches too much television."

Vik, who thought television was responsible for half of the sin and most of the crime in the world, kept abreast of all the programs, and watched those he found the most offensive.

Now, Marti and Vik headed for their unmarked Dodge. Vik

got in on the passenger side. Letting her drive had been his first major concession. He'd been married for twenty-seven years and his wife still didn't have a driver's license.

When they returned to the precinct, Vik got two cans of Mellow Yellow from the vending machine. Marti went to the coffeepot and tipped it to get the dregs at the bottom.

Vik opened his file drawer and extracted some report forms. He selected two pencils with the anticipation of one who loved filling out forms. He was the only cop she had ever met who never complained about the paperwork.

She preferred to write down her impressions in elaborate, informal detail, a work habit that always annoyed Vik, who thought everyone should be as concise as he was. She took out a legal-sized yellow pad.

The hit-and-run victim was still unidentified. His death, the Price woman, and the two fire victims made it four cases assigned to them in a week. It must have been some kind of a record for Lincoln Prairie.

"Vik, if Price walked to the park last Thursday, she could have passed the clinic."

"Yeah, kid, I know. Don't make too much of it yet, huh? We'll canvass the neighborhood tomorrow, see if anything useful turns up."

Frowning, she picked up a pencil. As soon as she finished these reports she could go home.

Her kids called the street they lived on the gingerbread village. All of the houses were roomy brick Tudors in varying shades of brown. Unlike the street they had lived on in Chicago, the houses weren't crowded together. They had wide lawns with hedges and rosebushes, and evergreens instead of fences separated one house from another.

She yawned. At least she didn't have to worry about Theo and Joanna. When she had decided to move here, her friend Sharon had been divorced for almost a year. Sharon had been teaching full time and waitressing part time to support herself and her daughter, Lisa. Now that Marti and Sharon shared the house and split the expenses, Sharon didn't have to work two jobs. She could be at home with the kids after school and during the summer. The arrangement was working out well.

Vik opened his second can of pop. "I wish the hell they'd do their killing during normal working hours," he said. "Damned inconsiderate keeping us up until 2:30 in the morning."

"Lack of planning on their part," Marti agreed.

"Poor planning, hell. They do it on purpose." He drank some of the pop. "Just what we need, a John Doe to go along with our Jane Doe. What the hell did someone do, send their little girl to the store and forget she was gone? We'd better get out of here. Petrosky's probably got the autopsies scheduled for daybreak. Maybe when we come in we'll at least have an ID on the hit-and-run."

"Maybe," she agreed. Probably someone local.

9

When the telephone rang, Marti groped for the receiver. Squinting, she glanced at the clock: 6:10. She groaned. Most mornings she woke ready, even eager to get up. Then there were days like this.

The telephone was under the bed. "Yeah."

It was the coroner, Janet Petrosky. "MacAlister, I've got two autopsies scheduled at seven. Danny Jones, possible vehicular homicide—"

"We got an ID on the hit-and-run?"

"Fingerprint and photo match. Not local. No next of kin located. Also Ruth Price. Cyprian is doing the Jones PM." Janet sneezed. She sounded like everything from her neck up was congested. "Damned allergies. This makes four bodies and at least two homicides in a week. Are we having a crime wave?"

"No. Not yet." She closed her eyes.

"Jessenovik still objecting to female officers viewing the remains of nude males?"

"Yeah."

Janet laughed. "That Jessenovik's been an anachronism since birth. It's about time he's had to work with someone who doesn't believe a woman should walk six paces behind him." She sneezed again. "Well, see you in forty minutes, MacAlister. Two autopsies and I'm off to the allergist."

Marti ordered her eyes to remain open and got up. By choice, hers was the smaller of the two rooms available when she'd moved in with the kids. She didn't want to sleep in a room large enough for two people. A single bed was pushed against one wall with a window, and a large old dresser with claw feet took up most of the space along the opposite wall. Framed pictures of Marti and Johnny and the kids crowded the dresser. There was an old black-and-white glossy snapshot of her parents in a pewter frame.

Everything she had worn since Sunday was tossed on a chair by the other window. Blouses in an untidy pile on the seat, slacks folded on the creases and hung over the back. Except for court appearances, when a navy blue skirt and blazer seemed more appropriate, she always wore slacks and service oxfords on the job. Sometimes she was teased about always being ready for a pursuit, but in Chicago chasing suspects had often been part of her daily routine.

Janet Petrosky was a stickler for promptness, so Marti showered and dressed quickly. She threw the beige bedspread over her rumpled sheet and listened for a click as she closed the door on her way out. Her room was always a mess, but she didn't want everyone to see how long it had been since she had vacuumed and straightened up.

By eight o'clock she was standing outside the coroner's facility. The doctor scheduled to perform the Price PM had been late, so Vik was still inside. She was glad that the Jones autopsy was over. Cold place, and not just because of the air conditioning. Cinder-block walls painted white, stainless steel tables and instruments, bright lights. And the smell. Even though she always put a little Vicks in her nostrils, either the odor or the memory of the first time she smelled it made her think of the old stockyards in Chicago where they slaughtered animals when she was a kid. It was already hot outside, and for a minute, as she stood in the bright sunlight, she felt goosebumps on her arms and shivered.

Danny Jones had looked awful lying on that table, even before his clothes were removed. Glass and pebbles embedded in his face and scalp. His nose and at least a dozen facial bones smashed. Whoever did it had been more than a little angry with him. He had a bruise around the intact eye that Dr. Cyprian had said Jones had received at least two days before he died.

After looking at his body—the abdomen one massive bruise, bones protruding from his right leg—watching him being opened up didn't make her feel queasy, until they discovered that he had ingested some Twinkies just before he died.

Vik liked Twinkies. She ought to buy him a pack, wait until he was eating them, and then describe what they looked like fifteen minutes into the digestive process. Trouble was, she might be the only one who got sick.

She stopped at the precinct and picked up a copy of Jones's rap sheet. Danny Montana Jones, age twenty. He had been arrested in May in Louisville, Kentucky, for armed robbery. He was held for twenty-eight days and released when the charges were dropped. There were no prior arrests, at least not as an adult. The only relatives on record were his parents, both deceased. Jones had been arraigned within a week after his arrest and the case had proceeded as far as a pretrial investigation. No telling why he had come here.

At 8:50 A.M., Marti pulled into the parking lot in front of the temporary quarters for the Lakeshore Clinic. The one-story building was only two blocks from the burned-out clinic and zoned for business. There were no other cars parked outside. Office hours began at nine-thirty. She was hoping to catch Dr. Edwards before his patients began arriving.

She hadn't spoken with Edwards since the night of the fire. The arson investigation had confirmed that the fire was deliberately set, and indicated that the building was insured for replacement value only. There had been no changes or increases in the policy since Edwards purchased the place. He reported that all financial records had been destroyed, but there was no evidence to indicate that he had any motive for committing the crime.

A light blue Hyundai pulled up in front of the clinic and an older woman got out. She was short and plump, with skin the color of walnuts. Marti watched as she searched through a large handbag. She had to be Mrs. Johnson, Dr. Edwards's daytime receptionist. She had been at a church function in Racine the night of the fire.

The woman was getting ready to unlock the door when Marti approached. "Mrs. Johnson?"

"Yes."

"Morning, ma'am. I'm Detective MacAlister." She showed the woman her shield. "I'm investigating the fire. Stopped by to talk with the doctor but it looks like he's not here yet. May I come in?"

"Why, certainly." Mrs. Johnson smiled and blinked. "Doctor should be here in the next twenty minutes or so."

Inside, the place smelled of new carpeting and fresh paint. Marti followed Mrs. Johnson down a short, unlit hall into a reception area. After one look at the molded plastic chairs she decided to stand.

Mrs. Johnson slipped into a pink-and-blue-striped smock and busied herself at her desk. "Sure wish I could help, but I wasn't here that night."

"Looks like you've been busy getting this place opened up."

Mrs. Johnson smiled. "Oh yes, what with so many of our records destroyed. It took me 'til Monday to get things in hand. There's a lot of information we'll never get back, but we'll be able to make do." She patted a stack of folders and seemed pleased with her efforts. "I sure hope you hurry up and find whoever did it. Terrible thing."

Marti took out the morgue photograph of the unidentified girl so that Mrs. Johnson could get a look at it before the doctor arrived. "Have you ever seen this young woman?"

Mrs. Johnson took the picture and studied it. "Never saw her that I can remember. Certainly not at the clinic. Doctor said it wasn't one of his girls." She returned the snapshot. "Dear Lord, you still don't know who she is, do you? Some poor woman somewhere is wondering what happened to her baby." She shook her head. "No. I'm sorry. I'd remember her." She dabbed her eyes with a Kleenex.

"Perhaps you could answer a few questions while we wait for the doctor. Just background information."

Mrs. Johnson hesitated. "Well, I suppose that would be all right."

"How well did you know Teresa Martinez?"

"Such a shame it was Teresa. But the Lord knows what he's doing, I suppose. So nice, polite. Carried herself well. Not at all like that friend of hers, Carmen."

Carmen Rodriguez was the other evening receptionist.

"Why did Dr. Edwards need two part-time receptionists in the evening, Mrs. Johnson?"

"Well, Doctor hired Carmen. Poor man, how was he to know she wasn't reliable? Carmen took advantage of him, took advantage of Teresa too. Teresa was the one who needed the job, poor girl, helping her widowed mother. From what Teresa said, I think Carmen just showed up when she needed some spending change."

"Why wasn't the Rodriguez girl fired?"

"Goodness, no. Doctor wouldn't do a thing like that."

The missing records were a nagging loose end. Edwards claimed to have lost all history of financial transactions and most of his patient records—diagnoses, treatments, prescriptions, referrals. It was as if, before the fire, Dr. Edwards hadn't practiced in Lincoln Prairie at all.

At the request of the arson investigator, Mrs. Edwards, who was an accountant and kept the books for her husband, had agreed to reconstruct as much of the information as possible. That would be based on existing documentation, such as income tax returns, and wouldn't be as accurate as the original documents and computer files.

"Doctor Edwards told me you helped his wife with the bookkeeping."

"Why, yes." Mrs. Johnson clasped her hands together

tightly. "The clinic is closed the last Wednesday afternoon of every month. And I use this little computer hardly bigger than a briefcase. I just take care of the bills—what the doctor owes on one disk, what people owe him on the other."

"And the doctor's wife helps."

"No, not exactly. She showed me how to use it and all. But she takes care of the checks, pays the bills, makes the deposits. And she comes in one Sunday a month to do the inventory." She frowned. "Even counts the Band-Aids. Nuisance, keeping track of them. 'You used three Band-Aids for each patient,' she'll say. Of course I know she's exaggerating, but I never worked for anybody who counted like that."

"The diskettes you used. Did you keep a duplicate set someplace else? Do you have a copy?"

"Doctor had one," Mrs. Johnson said. "In his desk, like I had mine. We didn't—you never think something like this will happen."

"Would his wife have copies too?"

"No, I don't think so."

The doctor had told Marti a similar story, but she didn't believe that there wasn't another set of diskettes outside the office. Vik, who was as meticulous about keeping records as the doctor's wife was about counting Band-Aids, made copies of many things in triplicate. And the doctor had better reasons for keeping records than that pack rat Jessenovik. It didn't make sense.

The door opened before she could ask any more questions.

Mrs. Johnson looked past Marti. "Doctor Edwards." She sounded relieved.

Marti turned. "Morning, Doctor."

As she spoke, his frown was replaced by the grave, solemn expression she remembered from the night of the fire.

10

Marti stepped into Edwards's office and closed the door. She got a whiff of his cologne, more pungent than sweet. Something citrusy. "My first appointment is due in ten minutes," he said. "I wasn't expecting you." He sounded like a radio announcer.

"I need to ask you a few more questions."

"Then please do so as expeditiously as possible. I hope you're making some progress," he said. "We've been busy opening this place. I haven't had time to inquire."

His office looked like he hadn't finished moving in. Maybe it was the walls—bare, no diplomas, no license. Lost in the fire, maybe. When people deliberately had their businesses torched they tended to move out everything valuable or important beforehand.

Information on the insurance claims indicated that Edwards had expensive taste. Thick plum and gray carpeting had been installed in this office, very different from the thin brown stuff in the waiting room. There were brass lamps and a coatrack, chairs upholstered in gray leather.

"Why did you hire Carmen Rodriguez?"

He raised his eyebrows. "Carmen? She answered an ad. Mrs. Johnson didn't want to work evenings."

"Why did you take on the Martinez girl too?"

He began toying with a mechanical pencil. "Actually, I didn't interview or hire her. Carmen called in sick one night, said she had a friend who could fill in for her. Teresa was competent, reliable."

Marti had attended the wake and the funeral. Teresa's mother had wept unconsolably. Her fiancé had been red-eyed and silent. The doctor had seemed ill at ease during the wake and stayed less than five minutes. He did not attend the funeral mass.

"Was Carmen competent and reliable too?"

He shrugged.

"Why didn't you let her go?"

Another shrug. "As long as one of them was here . . . no need to alienate my Hispanic patients by firing anyone."

Marti expected him to ask about the unidentified victim, if only to see if he knew who she was. She decided not to mention her unless Edwards did.

"The front door was locked the night of the fire. Should it have been?"

He took a step back, folded his arms. "Yes. I would have unlocked it when I came in."

"And you should have been the first one to arrive?"

"Yes."

"How did Carmen and Teresa get in?"

"Through the back. And no, there was no particular reason for that. They just did."

The fire had begun near the back door. Downstairs, there was also the side door she and Vik had used last Saturday. "You had recently changed the locks?"

"Yes." He shifted, brushed at his sleeve with manicured fingertips. "Expensive, but necessary. Teresa had lost her keys. I gave everyone a new set of keys right away."

She didn't tell him that Teresa's new key didn't fit the front door.

"Doctor, how do the clients you serve in the evenings differ from those who come here during the day?"

"More working women. Fewer pregnancies. Most want a convenient place for an annual exam. Not much follow-up. There is no other gynecologist in this part of town, and those on the fringe of this area don't have office hours at night."

"Should you have been there when the fire started? Did you leave unexpectedly?"

"No. I wasn't there, didn't need to be there that early. I did stay a little later than usual after my afternoon appointments. Then I went over to the fast-food place on Webster and Sherman. Ordered a salad from the take-out window. I ate in the car."

He seemed like a person who would eat something healthy. "Nobody was expecting you to be at the clinic at the time it was torched?"

"No. The girls were supposed to get there by 6:45, but they never got there sooner than seven. Appointments started at 7:15."

"That right-to-life group had been passing out literature near your clinic every day."

"Yes, and I've received anonymous threatening letters as well. The arson investigator has them."

There had been four letters. Words cut out of a newspaper, no traceability. Arson was satisfied that they were all sent by the same person.

"They've been pressuring area hospitals to stop abortion on demand for over a year now, with some results. Yours is the only private practice they've targeted. Any reason for that?"

"No. I do perform abortions at three hospitals, but no surgical procedures are performed here."

"Any special reason why not?"

"No. I prefer doing them at a hospital. For insurance reasons. Mrs. Johnson has nurse's-aide experience. That's adequate. If I did anything more in the office, I'd need a registered nurse. Besides, what's needed is a convenient place for routine, preventive health care. I intended to bring in a pediatrician next year, then open a pharmacy on the first floor. I'm not sure what I'm going to do now."

He checked the time on his Rolex. "Look, this is a depressed area, with poor, ignorant women who don't need a bunch of do-gooders telling them how to stay poor and ignorant by having another baby every year." He spoke without raising his voice or showing any emotion. "What do you expect these religious zealots to do, picket their own doctors? Their cheerleader, college-prep, honor-roll daughters visit elderly aunts or spend long weekends in Florida or California when they get abortions."

"Is there any reason why anyone else might have wanted to set that fire?"

"No. And I'm late for my first appointment." He made no mention of the unidentified girl.

When Marti got back to the precinct, Vik was at his desk.

"What's in that evidence bag?" she asked.

He dumped out the contents. "Jones's property," he said.

She walked over to his desk. A black wallet, leather, worn; half a Hershey's bar and a Snickers wrapper; fifty-seven cents. She looked in the wallet. Three one-dollar food stamps, a five-dollar bill.

"No driver's license, no Social Security card, no photographs," she said. "No phone numbers. No addresses."

"Not a hell of a lot of anything," Vik agreed.

"No next of kin, yet. Both parents dead."

"County will probably end up burying him."

"Too bad we have no way to find out if there's a juvenile record. Courts shouldn't be able to keep them sealed."

She'd feel better about the death of the orphaned man if she had proof that he mugged little old ladies and took candy from kids.

"We found the hit-and-run vehicle," Vik told her.

"That fast? I'm impressed."

"It could have taken weeks if it wasn't for Lupe Torres. One of her snitches suggested we check out some old man on her beat. Seems he leaves his car parked in his garage with the keys under the mat. People just take the car, bring it back, and leave either a little gas in the tank or some cash under the mat.

Evidence techs are over at his place now—they got a match with paint traces found at the scene. We're checking to see if we've got any open files involving the same type of vehicle. That old man needs to be locked up for being stupid."

"Or smart," Marti said. "He probably made a nice piece of change and had a full tank of gas most of the time."

Marti filled Vik in on Jones's injuries, then on her conversation with the doctor. "I wanted him to ask about that little girl," she admitted. "I was disappointed when he didn't."

"Why, because he's a doctor? He's got a lot on his mind right now, too."

"I suppose. What have you got on Ruth Price?"

"She died of a compression fracture. There were three wounds, though, not one. And scalp abrasions as if her hair had been pulled. The flatiron was being used as a doorstop. She could have been pushed, and hit her head when she fell. But someone slammed her head into that thing again and again." He slapped the palm of one hand against the other twice. "No witnesses, no fingerprints. No known enemies. Nothing. That sure as hell narrows it down. What do you say we question everyone within a fifteen-block radius?"

Marti's stomach rumbled, and she remembered that she hadn't eaten anything that morning. There were some doughnuts by the coffeepot—one honey-dipped and half a chocolate. A little dried out, but still edible.

11

By one o'clock Marti and Vik were talking with the owner of the car that hit Danny Jones.

"Folks just call me Old Tom," he said, giving them a gap-toothed smile. His plaid shirt hung on him as if it had belonged to a larger man.

Old Tom didn't recognize Danny Jones from the morgue shot. "Car mostly stays in the garage," he explained. "Ain't got much use for it no more."

His hand trembled as he held out the photo. "Got arthritis, don't drive no more than what I have to. Grandkids always come by wantin' to use it. Jus' leave the keys for 'em so's they won't come waking me up."

"It seems like a lot of people in the neighborhood know that the car is available," Vik said.

"Needs my rest," the old man said.

"Lot of damage to the front," Vik told him. "The grill and the hood are bent up, headlight's out. Got insurance to cover it?"

"Have to see," the old man said. "Got whatever the state says I gotta have on it. That's all."

"If we find out that car's been involved in anything else, we might consider you an accessory," Vik warned. "Better watch who you give those keys to from now on."

Next, they canvassed within a two-block radius of the fire-gutted clinic. As they progressed, it didn't look as if they were going to discover anything new.

When they neared the clinic, Vik took the liquor store just down the street, the only one in the city with a drive-up window.

Marti went into a small grocery store on the corner, separated from the clinic by a vacant lot.

Joe was a short, dark-haired Iranian who passed himself off as Hispanic. He spoke fluent Spanish and had kept the previous owner's name, Jose Lopez, on the door. Marti was certain that despite Joe's caution, nobody in the neighborhood cared about his heritage.

Joe nodded and smiled a lot. "Yes ma'am. Certainly. I will look at the pictures again. The other officers, the ones in uniform, they show me the pictures too."

She stood on the customers' side of the counter. Candy had to be a big seller. There was an incredible variety, much of it costing a nickel. She hadn't seen anything like it since she was a kid. She could almost taste the jawbreakers and Mary Janes.

Joe looked at the photographs of R.D., both dead girls, and a few anonymous perps currently doing time in Joliet. She had added morgue shots of Danny Jones and Ruth Price and a mug shot of Glodine, one of the women associated with R.D. who had been arrested once for prostitution.

Joe identified Teresa and Carmen. He hesitated when he came to the snapshot of Price. "This is the woman who was killed last night?"

"Yes."

He seemed to want to tell her something. She waited.

"I have seen her."

"Was she a customer?"

Again he hesitated.

"She's dead," Marti reminded him. "What can you tell me?"

"This old woman, she comes through the alley. On Thursday. Other old ones come too."

He seemed uneasy and moved to the rear of the store. He stopped at a long case filled with fruit and vegetables. Everything looked fresh except for some produce stacked on an unrefrigerated shelf.

"On Thursday, what was delivered on Monday I sell at half

price." He pointed to the unrefrigerated produce, a little wilted but not spoiled. "What is left when I am ready to close I put out with the garbage. In a box, separate. The old ones come. They take it.

"I could still sell," he said, "but I put out. In my country, there is hunger. Here there are so many rules. Is wrong, illegal that I put it out? I do not put it with the rest of the garbage, I keep it separate. The old ones know."

"It's okay," she assured him, unwilling to get involved with health-code violations. "You can put out whatever you want and package it any way you want to." At least she thought so. "There are soup kitchens, churches, and other places that give out food."

"Yes, yes. But the old ones, they come here. They do not have to beg. Is there and is free and nobody to pity them. Is almost like shopping." He handed back Ruth Price's photo. "This one, she liked oranges. And sometimes a peach. They do not take more than they need. Is legal?"

"It's okay," she repeated. She didn't tell him that she was glad he put the produce out, glad that Ruth Price got a few oranges every week and had eaten one last night before she died.

12

Marti didn't leave the precinct until five-thirty. She had promised Theo and Joanna that she'd go jogging with them this evening, but she had to see one of her snitches first.

Her snitch, Doretta Eldridge, was a preacher of sorts. She had dropped out of school without learning to read and had spent the next sixteen years getting drunk or high. When she stopped using, she began carrying a Bible and preaching downtown, standing on a corner the commuters passed on their way to and from the train station.

After she was clean and sober for six months, her parents were so glad that she wasn't abusing drugs or alcohol anymore that they let her live at home and use their garage for church services. They lived three blocks from where Jones was killed, and Doretta knew the neighborhood well. Marti was hoping she had heard of Danny Jones.

She pulled up in front of a yellow bungalow. Petunias grew in a wide border across the front of the house and cascaded from window boxes. The garage door was open. Inside, five people sat on folding chairs, their backs to the garden tools that were lined up against one wall. For Doretta this was a big crowd. Marti wasn't sure why they came, but on another night while she waited to speak with Doretta, a woman said to her, "Isn't it wonderful, the way the Spirit speaks through her, praise God. When the Lord sends an interpreter, we'll understand."

Doretta was thirty-two and looked at least fifty. She wasn't wrinkled or old in any ordinary way, just used up by her drugs of choice. She paced back and forth, Bible open, shoulders hunched forward. "And God said, 'Roll back the waters of the Jordan,' and the children of Daniel walked over Nebechedonazer's chariots and were drowned."

Marti could never make a bit of sense out of Doretta's sermons and didn't think Doretta knew what she was talking about, either. She seemed to like the sound of the phrases strung together. It sure wasn't anything like the well-thought-out sermons of Marti's own minister.

"And the Lord told Hezekiah, 'Send Edom to the Philistines whilst I gather cedar out of the desert.' "

Marti got a folding chair and sat in the driveway, checking her watch. It was five minutes to six. Service should be about over. It seemed like another half hour before people began to leave, but it was only six minutes.

Doretta greeted Marti. "Sister Mac. So good of you to come." She pulled up a chair, wiping sweat from her dark forehead with the back of her hand. "Whew. Spirit been movin' today. Praise God."

Doretta had experienced her conversion after being beaten and stabbed in a barroom brawl a couple of years ago. When she was released from the hospital, she began calling the precinct with information about liquor stores where alcohol was sold to minors and schoolyards where drugs were sold to kids.

Once Doretta began to quote Scripture, she lost whatever credibility she could have had with the police. The dispatcher put her down as a crank caller and sent out the greenest recruits to interview her. As a prank, Marti was sent out here her second day on the job. Unlike the others, Marti liked Doretta, and had asked to have the calls referred to her every time.

Through Marti, Doretta passed along the names of Satan's helpers to the narcs. Between the two of them, they were doing a reasonable job of keeping drugs away from the two elementary schools closest to Doretta's house, and their information had resulted in the arrest of a pusher at one of the junior high schools. Several liquor-store owners had been issued warnings about selling to minors, and two bars had been temporarily closed.

Doretta had a lazy eye. The left eye looked straight at Marti while the right eye tried to catch up. "Sure was good of you to bring Brother Malcolm to the Lord, Sister."

Malcolm was a thirteen-year-old Marti had helped get into a drug treatment program. She thought of her own two kids at home waiting for her, getting impatient, or perhaps already disappointed because they didn't think she was coming.

"Got a few more names for you, Sister. Devil just trampling down the lilies and the sparrows what feeding on the chaff in the fields."

Marti took down the names, promised to look into it.

"So good to see one of our own wearin' that badge, Sister. Letting these chil'ren see they own is here to help 'em and not jes' lock 'em up."

This was one of the reasons Marti liked her. Doretta assumed she wanted to help people.

"Jacob's children, coming out of the fiery furnace with the apocalypse pestilence burning behind them."

Her children, ready to go jogging at the forest preserve. "Do you know anyone named Danny Jones?"

Doretta frowned with concentration, biting on the corner of her lower lip. "Got hisself killed last night. Lived over on Eureka."

"Right." Marti spoke calmly. "That rooming house that had the fire last year?" she guessed.

"That be the one."

Marti thought again of Joanna and Theo waiting for her while she checked out the rooming house, but maybe it wouldn't take long.

"Know anything about Jones?"

"Pilate's centurion, ridin' the golden calf."

Doretta's description of a thief. Jones had been arrested for

61

armed robbery. Had he been stealing while he was here? "I need to know more about him."

"Serpent struck down the wicked seeking justice."

Now what the hell did that mean?

"Goin' to fornicate with Satan's harlot when the Lord struck him."

"Fornicate with who?"

"Don't know who she was."

Isaac had heard a woman's voice last night.

"You'll call if you hear anything else?"

"Sure will, Sister. Fire rises out of the pit to consume the children and them what's comin' now pour their blood into the cup of indignation."

Doretta accepted a small donation to the church, and Marti almost ran to her car. She put in a call to have Vik meet her at the Eureka Street address. She had shown the landlord Jones's photo. She'd have his building checked for code violations first thing Monday morning. Maybe next time he'd be more cooperative.

She checked her watch. The forest preserve closed when it got dark. If there just weren't any more delays . . .

13

When Marti arrived at the rooming house, Vik was waiting for her.

"The landlord recognized Jones's photo this time," he said. "Jones used the name Smith, and was renting by the week."

Jones's room was at the rear of a dark hallway, and his few belongings were strewn about the floor: jeans, a denim jacket, red briefs. Crumpled candy-bar wrappers and three unopened cans of cola were the only indications that he ate here.

A quick check of the winos and junkies in residence confirmed what Marti expected. Nobody knew anything. Nobody could identify the morgue shot. An evidence technician was coming in as they left. Marti didn't expect her to find anything, either.

"How'd you get the address?" Vik asked.

"Doretta Eldridge," she said, trying not to sound like she was gloating.

Vik jammed his hands in his pockets and stomped to his car without saying anything else.

Theo and Joanna were waiting on the front steps when Marti got home. She changed into blue shorts and Nikes and drove to the forest preserve in Johnny's 1956 Bel Air. She had found a mechanic who loved the car almost as much as Johnny had, and he had given it a tune-up a couple of days ago. Everything sounded good.

"Forty-five minutes to sunset," she announced as they walked the gravel path to the trail.

"Three laps," Joanna said.

"Two, maybe," Marti countered. "I'm tired."

Thanks to Theo, Marti knew more about the local flora and fauna than she wanted to. Green and amber waves of grain had lost their anonymity and became Indian hemp and squirrel grass. A restful pastel blur seemed a little less picturesque now that she could identify yellow rosinweed and pink and white Culver's root. Still, something about being able to name the flowers was beginning to please her.

Theo had jogged ahead and was squatting near a clump of purple blossoms. As she approached him, Marti could see his father in the cleft of his chin and the perfect arch of his eyebrows. Theo had Johnny's dark eyes and the serious expression that seldom gave way to laughter, and almost never revealed what he was thinking.

Beside her, Joanna set the pace. Both children ran much the same way as they did everything else: Theo in fits and starts, stopping to look at everything along the way; Joanna, her goal determined, almost oblivious to everything else.

"You ready for the party tomorrow night?" Marti asked.

"I guess so."

"Excited?"

"Not really."

Marti glanced at her daughter. In profile Joanna looked just like momma, the contours of her round face soft and full, her mouth generous and half smiling. One long, thick auburn braid hung down her back, swinging as she jogged. Joanna was already tall, large boned, and well developed. Even though she was interested in one of the football players, Joanna had gone unescorted to her Frosh Hop and the spring Turnabout. This summer, Sharon's daughter was dating, but Joanna was not.

"Who's going to be there? Want me to blue-shirt anyone?"

"Oh, ma. You won't have to play cop. What about Theo's camping trip? Are you going to let him go?"

Puzzled, she let Joanna change the subject. "I haven't come up with a good reason to say no."

"He went once with Dad."

"Your dad didn't even like Grant Park after he came back from Vietnam."

"But he did go camping that one time with the church Scout troops."

She thought about that for a minute. "I think he needed to prove something." Or maybe remember something. Or figure out how to forget it. Johnny had been having nightmares again before he went to that campground in Michigan. They had stopped when he came back.

"He'd probably want Theo to go."

"Probably," Marti agreed.

"We can visit Dad's grave just once without him."

"I know."

After they left the jogging trail, Marti drove Theo and Joanna home. She took a quick shower and changed into a pantsuit with a ruffled white blouse.

Hungry, she shared a salad with Joanna: carrots, alfalfa sprouts, spinach, raisins, sunflower seeds, and a little feta cheese. Theo took one look at it, said "Yuck," and helped himself to barbecued chicken and potato salad. Marti thought his reaction was sensible and wanted to do the same, but yielded to Joanna's preoccupation with cholesterol, hypertension, clogged arteries, and heart attacks. While Joanna might not be able to control whether or not her surviving parent got shot on the job, Marti had to smile at her daughter's efforts to ensure her continued good health.

When Marti went back outside the sky was a cloudless inky blue with a three-quarter moon. The stars seemed close. A light breeze blew cool from the northwest, and the neighbor's rose-bushes scented the air.

She had decided to take Johnny's car to the ravine where they had found Jones's body last night. Shining her flashlight down into the darkness, she was just able to make out the thin stream of slow-moving water far below. Lincoln Prairie River, according to Vik.

It was dark here. There wasn't much traffic. No people. There was a bar two blocks away. The Public Aid Office was nearby, but closed, as were four secondhand stores, a theater, a bakery, and a grocery store. Years ago, before the malls were built, this was a thriving business district.

Gravel crunched as she walked away from the edge of the ravine toward the paved parking lot. It was several hundred feet to the Dumpster and the house where she hoped to find Isaac. If she was lucky, Isaac wouldn't have hooked up with his friend Dare yet. This late in the month Isaac wouldn't have the money to get drunk, but Dare usually picked up a little work riding a garbage truck a couple of days a week and had enough change in his pocket to keep the two of them supplied with cheap wine.

Unlike Isaac, who was almost a recluse, Dare was a social drinker. One swig of liquor and Dare had to talk, even if he just talked to himself. One night last week Marti had parked near a corner and watched Dare take half an hour to walk a block because he had to stop and say something to everyone he passed. It occurred to her then that Dare might pick up a few odd bits of useful information along the way.

That was when she began to think about cultivating Isaac as a snitch. She didn't like Dare and didn't like working with a snitch she didn't respect. But Dare talked to Isaac for hours, and Isaac never forgot anything he heard. She would have to find out if he would repeat it.

Vik thought she was crazy because she wanted to have some respect for her informants. Johnny had understood. They had been raised to respect everyone. "There but for the grace of God . . ." their parents would say. Her mother would add, "Bad times ain't that far away. Ain't none of us goin' far enough in this life to be gettin' uppity."

She spotted Isaac now, sitting on the back step of the house that had become his summer home. Most of the plywood that once covered the windows had been pried loose. The gas and electricity had been turned off when the place was condemned, but she'd heard there was running water.

As far as she could tell, Isaac changed his clothes once a month. Next week, when he picked up his SSI check at the post office, Isaac would have a hot bath at the YMCA, deck himself out in a new pair of jeans and a shirt, find himself a whore, and then begin the slow process of getting dirty and smelly again.

"How's it goin', Isaac?" She tested the porch rail. When it didn't give, she leaned against it, positioning herself upwind of Isaac.

"Officer Mac." He didn't sound like he'd been drinking. Despite the cool evening breeze, sweat made his brown face shiny. Maybe Dare was running late and he needed a drink. His rib cage was outlined by a tight, olive drab T-shirt. His beard was shaggy and flecked with gray. He had told her he was thirty-nine. It was hard to believe he was only a year older than she was.

"Remember anything else about that hit-and-run last night?"

He kicked at the glass shards and pebbles that paved the alley. "Isaac don't see nothin'," he reminded her. "Don't never see nothin'."

"Remember hearing anything else?"

"Nothin' more'n that car like I tol' you."

He cocked his head to one side as if he were listening to something.

"You sure that's all?" she prompted.

"Lot of stuff goin' on 'round here. Try not to hear most of it."

"Could be something important."

"S'pose so." He looked down the alley. "Most of what happens 'round here ain't nothin' but a bunch of foolishness."

"Might not be as foolish as it seems."

Isaac checked the alley again. "Jes' like a woman. Never

satisfied with nothin'. Always wantin' more. Make you better at this than a man." He gave a short, phlegm-filled giggle. "Whole lot of cops never even thought about askin' ol' Isaac nothin' 'til you come along, Officer Mac." He laughed again.

She wondered what he was thinking, how much more he had heard over the years and never spoke of.

"Got a cigarette on you?"

She kept a pack in her purse although she didn't smoke. "Here. Need a match?"

"Got that." After several attempts with trembling hands he got the flame close enough to the cigarette to light it. He sucked in noisily, then turned away to exhale. "Hear it wasn't nothin' but a boy what got killed."

He waved the cigarette in an agitated arc, pointing toward the spot where Jones had been hit. "Car hit him, he go *umph* jes' like someone let the air out of him. Die like a dog the way that car come at him. Die like an ordinary dog."

Marti didn't think Isaac had been close enough to hear that much, but she was impressed with his vehemence. No telling why this bothered him. "Need you to do a little more listening for me."

"Eh?" He twisted his body, sitting so that he was facing away from her, exhaling smoke.

She didn't think he was going to like being a snitch. She let him sit there for a few minutes thinking about it, hoped he'd remember last winter—how cold it was, and the times she got him into the Salvation Army shelter or sent a uniform to put him in jail for the night when the shelter was full, to keep warm and get a little food.

"Need to know if anyone is bringing little girls to town to turn tricks, Isaac. Runaways, most likely."

Isaac took a deep drag on the cigarette, averted his face, took another drag. After he flicked the glowing butt away from the steps, he said, "Isaac don't never see nothin'."

"But you hear real good. And I got a dead little girl on my hands with a momma somewhere worrying about her." She thought she was overdoing it, but Isaac seemed thoughtful. She had a hunch he had a soft spot somewhere. People who didn't say much often did.

"If I hear somethin'." A match flared as he lit up again. "S'pose if I do. Seein' as it's a kid."

"Thanks, Isaac. Shame for her to just be lying there, unclaimed."

"Like a suitcase in a bus terminal," Isaac said. He looked up at her, cigarette dangling from his mouth, and stared for a long minute as if he were gauging whether her request came from genuine concern or was just another kind of exploitation. "Isaac be listenin'," he said at last.

Recruiting snitches seldom made Marti feel good unless they volunteered, like Doretta. Isaac seemed like a decent enough person who just wanted to stay drunk, mind his own business, and leave most people alone to mind theirs.

As she walked back to her car, she felt lousy. She heard footsteps behind her and turned. It was Isaac, hands in his pockets, whistling. She waited until he caught up. When he didn't stop walking she fell in step beside him. The whistling stopped. He began to sing an old blues song she remembered from when she was a kid.

"Got women like little angels, every night they spread their wings." His voice was high pitched, thready, and off-key. "Little girls like little angels," he began, changing the words. "Ridin' 'round in birds with silver wings. Got a daddy and a momma, teach 'em how to fly and spread their wings."

He began whistling again, walking faster, turning in the general direction of the tavern. He didn't look back.

She sat in Johnny's Bel Air and thought about the changes Isaac had made with the words to the song. R.D. drove a gray Continental. That could be the silver bird. And "momma." A woman. Linda? Glodine? "Teaching them to fly," drugs. "Spread their wings" was an old sexual innuendo. Not a bad night's work, she decided, humming the song Isaac had sung.

14

By quarter to six Saturday
morning, Marti had already fried and eaten four strips of slab
bacon and two eggs sunny-side up. The kitchen was bright with
sunlight, and from outside she could hear the chatter of sparrows interrupted by the squawking of grackles. She hummed as
she spread pineapple jam on toast.

Sharon had decided to "brighten up" the house to relieve
her depression while she was going through her divorce. The
kitchen was painted a glossy yellow that screamed good morning no matter what time it was. The wall facing the backyard had
six tall, wide windows with a huge Boston fern hanging at each.
Marti found it impossible to feel depressed or remain irritable in
this room, and had avoided coming in here the first few weeks
after she moved in.

As Marti poured a second cup of coffee, Sharon clattered
into the kitchen on three-inch-high mules.

"And I suppose you're awake at this hour," Sharon said,
pushing at the kinky mass of hair that hung to her shoulders and
flopped on her forehead.

Sharon, just five feet tall and a scant hundred pounds, did
everything she could to create an illusion of density and height.
Her tentlike caftan, silky yards of turquoise, pink, and purple
stripes, swirled and settled into graceful folds as she stood in the
middle of the room.

"I don't believe this, Marti MacAlister. Daybreak on a Saturday morning in the middle of summer vacation and I'm standing, walking, talking, and feeling almost human." She looked

down at her feet and wiggled her toes as if to confirm that, then yawned. "There are days when I can't handle these walls. Color's all wrong unless you've had a decent night's sleep. Screams at you."

Marti smiled. There were days when she might not have gotten out of bed if it hadn't been for the welcoming warmth she found here.

Sharon continued to stand there, swaying. "How come you're so wide-awake? I don't know how you do it, girl, with the hours you keep when you're on a case."

"You get used to it." Marti poured her some coffee. "Want an eye-opener?"

"You make this?"

"Nobody else was up."

"Yuck," Sharon said without tasting it. Coffee sloshed on the floor as she went to the table and sat down, caftan billowing. "Looks like you added a little more water than usual to the coffee grounds. It moves when I tilt the cup."

"I like the way I make coffee."

"Me too, when I don't want to blink my eyes for the next twenty-four hours. That doesn't happen too often."

Marti wiped up the coffee Sharon had spilled on the floor. "Complain, complain. You need a night out, a little dancing."

"Why do you think I'm so tired? Mr. Wonderful dropped by after work last night. I don't think I got three hours' sleep."

Since her divorce, Sharon alternated between months of celibacy and an occasional brief affair. She seemed to prefer men she had nothing in common with, and had called each of the three she had dated since Marti had moved in "Mr. Wonderful."

"Is he still here?"

"Marti, of course not. We've got kids. I sent him home about three-thirty."

"Oh." Dating wasn't something that concerned Marti right now. She wasn't sure it ever would. For one thing, she had no idea of how to handle it as far as her kids were concerned. She did go out to dinner with Ben Walker once or twice a month, but they were just friends.

Sharon sighed. "He's not a bad dancer. In fact, if Mr. Wonderful's horizontal moves were half as good as his vertical moves I might be in love again, instead of bored stiff. Which is something else that would have been nice, something that stayed a little stiffer a little longer, or was just a little longer maybe." She laughed, a tinny sound without humor.

Marti had a hunch this guy wouldn't be around long enough for introductions. "Hungry?"

"Bacon smells good. Got up early to sneak a little cholesterol?"

"Ate the last two eggs, too. Thought you were going shopping yesterday."

"I did. With Joanna."

Marti laughed. "See, what did I tell you, girl? Food just disappears out of the basket when you take that child along."

Sharon ran her fingers through her tangled hair. "Lord, I couldn't believe it. By the time we got to the check-out I had skim instead of whole milk, two packs of pork chops were gone, and there were five packs of perch. And no eggs, even though I took two dozen out of the case. I don't know what happened to the ribs I was going to barbecue today but I'm going back to get more. From now on I'm taking my daughter and leaving yours at home. Lisa takes after me. She doesn't like anything she thinks might possibly be good for her."

Marti brought some toast and bacon to the table. "I threw out that orange juice. Tasted like it had turned."

"Girl, it had carrot juice in it. Joanna made it last night. I'll tell her it spilled. But thanks, I sure wasn't looking forward to having any."

Marti noticed the typewriter set up at one end of the table and debated about asking Sharon what cause she was involved with now. Last summer it was Greenpeace. A month after joining the force here, she had had to get Sharon out of jail when she was arrested for participating in a peace demonstration at a nearby military base. For a week Vik had acted as if she were consorting with a known felon.

In spite of herself, she said, "You're not getting mixed up with those antiabortionists picketing in front of the hospital, are you?"

"What pickets?"

Now she'd done it. Sharon would be organizing a counter-protest by noon. "The *News-Times* is ignoring them."

"Thank God. Ain't nobody telling me what I can or cannot do with my body. Two hundred years of that was more than enough. And 'black genocide' be damned. Ain't nobody but me gonna feed, shelter, or clothe any child I bring into this world."

Marti was against abortion for herself, but she felt the same way as Sharon did about it being legal.

"And I just can't handle Reverend Halloran's groupies," Sharon said. "I might be getting old or slow-witted or something, but I don't have much patience with 'em. 'Course I've taught some of their kids. They need to come to school more often instead of spending so much time marching in front of a hospital. They definitely need to worry more about the kids they've got than the ones that ain't been thought of yet. They'd probably get better results handing out condoms at their church services."

Sharon munched on the bacon. "I don't even think abortion is what we're really talking about anymore. Control maybe. Power. Men get scared to death if they think their women might be easin' up outta that missionary position. Some women get a little scared, too."

When Sharon spoke with this much anger edging her voice, it usually meant she had heard from her ex-husband. "So, how's good old Franklin these days?" Marti asked.

"Franklin's just fine. She's pregnant."

"She" was Franklin's second wife.

"Won't be no abortion there. Good old Franklin is taking me back to court to get his child-support payments reduced again. They get reduced any more and I'll be paying him. And the judge always agrees with him. He must think any woman dumb enough to get a divorce deserves to keep on getting screwed by the bastard afterwards. I had to wait six years to get pregnant, put Franklin through school first. Now me and my kid don't count."

Marti wasn't sure of what to say or how to help. Their marriages had been different. She always thought of Franklin as a taker. There might have been times when she wished Johnny wasn't so quiet, that he would talk to her more, but she had never felt used.

"When's your next court date?" she asked.

"Tuesday. And my attorney didn't sound optimistic."

"Sharon, get another lawyer."

"You've suggested that before, Marti. What's the difference?"

"Trust me."

"You know something I don't?"

Marti hesitated, then explained. "The chemistry isn't always right between a lawyer and a judge. Maybe that's part of the problem. Call the guy I suggested."

Sharon thought it over for a couple of minutes. "Okay, I'll try it. And I'll try not to get mad at you if this one is worse than the lawyer I've got. And, to get to the real reason why I dragged myself down here at the crack of dawn—Lisa and Joanna are having their party tonight. Think you could be here or stop in? Lisa can't wait to get all those young boys in here, but Joanna doesn't even seem interested. I thought she'd be making all kinds of health-food crap that would scare them away. But not one Jell-O mold and no extra fruit or veggies when we went shopping yesterday."

"Maybe she's not ready yet."

"At fifteen? Not ready? Honey, their hormones are screaming go! go! before they're twelve."

Marti didn't want to admit that she was concerned. "Let's

just wait and see what happens. No point in pushing her into something she's not ready for. She'll know when she wants to start fooling around with boys. If I get a reprieve this summer I'm not going to complain."

"I suppose," Sharon conceded. "What about Theo's camping trip?"

"We can talk about that tomorrow."

"I probably won't see you tomorrow. That's why I set the alarm this morning."

Marti gulped down the rest of her coffee and reached for her purse. Time she was leaving. "Theo's never gone camping before. Not really. No reason why he should now."

"Oh Marti, come on. We're just talking about a few days in the woods. Campfires, toasted marshmallows, burned hot dogs, poisonous mushrooms, starving mosquitoes, wild bears attacking the campers. We're not talking about abduction or child abuse."

"You know what day next Saturday is."

Sharon rubbed her eyes. "I know. Would have been Johnny's big four-zero. It's staring me in the face, too. Strange, not having Johnny around. He was as close to having a big brother, daddy, uncle, and male friend as I ever got. But Ben rented that cabin in March. Have you said anything to him? You must talk about something when you go out."

"Dinner once a month isn't 'going out,' and no, we haven't discussed anything as personal as our spouses."

"Thought you two were friends."

"We are." But Johnny and Ben's deceased first wife were still off limits. She didn't know why he had remarried so soon, or if his divorce from his second wife was final yet. "Dinner is more than enough. No need to get personal."

Sharon pushed her hair away from her forehead. "You mean that, don't you? Both of you mean that. Playing it safe from now on, huh? Playing it real safe. Sitting across from each other and jabbing at french fries a couple of times a month and discussing the weather, maybe, is enough."

"No french fries," Marti lied.

Sharon laughed. "Girl, I know you. No way you'd sneak up on a baked potato if there were some fries within a mile."

Marti grinned and slung her purse strap over her shoulder.

"You leaving already?"

"Roll call's in twenty minutes."

"But you're not even on duty today."

"Never know when you'll hear something of interest."

"You might hear something interesting right here," Sharon teased.

Marti refilled their cups and sat down again. She'd barely spent any time at home in over a week.

"You need to bring the job home every once in a while."

Marti shook her head. It was more a matter of understanding what the job was than discussing the particulars. She talked about her work more with Ben than she had with Johnny. Probably to avoid talking about anything else.

"Then you don't want to know anything about Reeva Edwards?" Sharon said.

"The doctor's wife? What do you know about her?"

"She was born right here in Lincoln Prairie."

"But she hasn't lived here in years."

"Girl, those old sisters at church are just going on about her like you wouldn't believe." Sharon began mimicking an old woman. " 'Why, honey, she done gone and got herself all that education, lef' her fam'ly, lef' her church, lef' town, and still ain't a bit more'n she always was, jus' one of them dirty Wrights.' "

"Why do they call her that?"

"Poor. Dirt poor. With fancy ideas."

"Nothing wrong with that, Sharon. Sounds like us."

"It seems wrong to a lot of folks if you don't take anyone with you and you don't come back. She comes from a big family and she's got too much not to help any of them."

Sharon cleared her throat, reverted to her old-lady voice. " 'Why, Miss High and Mighty ain't even spoke to her momma in the last ten years.' "

"What about the doctor?"

"I went to him one time," Sharon said. "The only black doctor in town, big deal. He doesn't ask you any questions. He doesn't talk at all. I could have left there with cancer of the everything and been none the wiser. I don't even think he knew my name when I walked out the door."

"He seems to have a large practice."

"I'm sure he does. He accepts anyone with a green card."

"He doesn't restrict his Public Aid patients? Everyone else does."

"Takes as many as he can get, even with Illinois so slow in paying. He's also open on Wednesdays, two Saturday mornings a month, and has evening clinic two nights a week. And his office is the only one in that part of town. So, if he's not too friendly, doesn't remember your name, and sells you his free samples—"

"He sells his free samples?"

"So?" Sharon seemed puzzled. "The pediatrician I used to take Lisa to sold us bottles of ampicillin. Cheaper than the pharmacy."

"Were they samples, too?"

"No, just regular bottles like you'd get at the drugstore. Edwards sells those little free samples, the kind other doctors give to you. That's no crime, is it?"

"No," Marti lied. Edwards could pull some solid time for that. It was a Federal offense.

15

At three-thirty Saturday afternoon, Marti was sitting in a brown Chevy, borrowed from the pound, watching R.D.'s house. It hadn't taken much to convince a neighbor that his garage was an ideal spot for this surveillance.

From where she was sitting she could look past the Chevy's crumpled right fender and see R.D.'s back door, his yard with the grass trimmed short and not one flower, and his garage, which was unattached and near the alley.

Vik had similar duty watching the front. It was Marti's idea. If R.D. didn't have an underaged girl inside and didn't get an urgent need to move her to a safer place, Marti was going to be the butt of a lot of bad jokes by Monday morning. She wasn't sure how much longer Vik would go along with her. Her two-way radio remained silent. R.D. was still at the pool hall where he'd been cueing up for the past two and a half hours.

She shifted and rotated her shoulders, feeling cramped even though the seat was pushed back. Her blouse was damp where she'd been leaning against the vinyl upholstery. It was muggy and overcast outside, and the stillness of the air in the garage made it seem even hotter. The owner of the garage was shellacking a table. The odor was almost nauseating in the heat.

Her throat felt dry, so she took another sip of flat, tepid Pepsi, careful not to drink enough to necessitate a trip to the john. Just three hours ago she had gone to the precinct, intending to write out a brief report and then head over to watch Joanna's softball game. Her plans had begun to fall apart as soon as she spoke to the desk sergeant, who pointed to a small holding room.

"Got a visitor, MacAlister. Martinez girl's brother."

Talking with relatives of the deceased wasn't something Marti looked forward to. She stood just inside the doorway, hoping this wouldn't take long. A stocky man at least a head shorter than she was paced the narrow distance between a table in the center of the room and a smudged pink wall. There were no windows.

"Mr. Martinez." She recognized him from his sister's funeral. He had cried throughout, wiping at his eyes and blowing his nose with a big white handkerchief.

As he turned now she could see a thatch of black hair curling just above the ribbed neckline of his T-shirt. Hair covered his arms. The beginnings of a pot gut bulged just above his belt.

He jabbed a short, stubby finger at the air. "You're the one who comes and upsets my mother."

"Someone had to tell her about your sister."

"And you still have not found out who kills my Teresita. Nine days now and you still do not know." There was just the slightest quaver in his voice. Maybe he had been close to his sister, or maybe he was just possessive and overprotective. Right now he seemed more frustrated than angry. "You think that because we are Hispanic you do not have to bother finding out who did this."

She didn't remind him that she was a minority too. "We're doing everything possible."

She pulled up a chair, wished she could read the newspaper someone had left folded on the table. Even yesterday's news seemed preferable to another recitation of Teresa Martinez's virtues.

"My Teresita was a good girl. Never any trouble from her. Never. It is Carmen who should have been there. Carmen who disrespects her parents and does nothing to help her sisters. Carmen who lives while my Teresita is dead."

She folded her arms. There were so many photographs of Teresa at her mother's apartment. On the tables, on the walls. Teresa, from toddler to teenager, always wearing elaborate organza and taffeta and satin dresses with ruffles and ribbons and bows. Her smile was always the kind you got when the photographer said, "Say cheese."

She let Mr. Martinez go on for a good five minutes about his little sister before interrupting. "We need to know who her friends were."

"I have told you."

"Teresa had to associate with someone besides those two girls she knew from church, the Rodriguez girl, and a fiancé she'd dated since high school."

"Her fiancé is the brother of my best friend. They are betrothed when she is sixteen. There was never any other man. And my Teresita is not friends with someone like Carmen Rodriguez."

"Then why did Carmen help Teresa get the job at the clinic?"

"They know each other from school, that is all. Carmen knows my Teresita will go in for her when she is too lazy to work but will not try to take the job away from her. My Teresita could never be like that Carmen, out all hours of the night, so many boyfriends, no help to her parents who are still in Mexico. She does not even send them a dime." He began pointing his thumb at his chest. "I raise Teresita when our father dies. I tell her it is okay that she work at the clinic. The doctor needs someone who speaks Spanish. She can help the women who come there. I take her pay, give her what she needs, put the rest into the bank for her husband when she marries. In December she was to be married, the day of our parents' anniversary. She was a good girl, my Teresita. Everything I tell her she does."

Marti tilted back in the chair. His boasting seemed arrogant.

"And if family planning was discussed at that clinic, Mr. Martinez? If contraceptives were prescribed? If the women who went there also went to the hospital to have abortions?"

He stood still for a few seconds, clenching his fists then spreading his fingers so wide his knuckles cracked. He looked as if he were about to paw the floor and charge at her. "That is not so. My Teresita would tell me of such a thing at once and I would never allow her to work at such a place."

"What if she was explaining contraceptive methods and abortion procedures when she was interpreting for the doctor?"

"Never! She is a good Catholic girl. Never would she do such a thing!"

"You couldn't allow or forbid something you knew nothing about."

"You speak lies!"

"It was a medical clinic, Mr. Martinez, not a chapel. Obstetrics and gynecology. What do you think went on there?"

"No! Dr. Edwards does not kill babies. Teresita tells me that herself."

"Dr. Edwards performs abortions at the hospital. The women come to the clinic first. If they spoke only Spanish, someone would have to explain to them."

"No!" he shouted. "No! Not my Teresita. She knows I would never permit it. You lie. You speak lies. She is dead and cannot speak for herself. You put lies in the mouth of a dead girl." Red-faced with rage, he rushed from the room.

Now, sitting in this hot garage, Marti wondered if the Martinez family believed everything they said about Teresa or if, for some reason, they needed to insist that she was perfect. Even if what they said about her was true, had the girl been happy or resentful? Had she felt compliant or coerced? She would have to find out more about the late Teresa Martinez from someone other than family members and her fiancé.

To stop the tingling sensation in her toes, Marti stretched her legs to the passenger side and jiggled her feet. There were no observable signs of occupancy at R.D.'s but Glodine had taken out a bag of garbage a few minutes ago. Linda had come to the back door. Whatever she said made Glodine hurry back inside. Marti's radio was quiet. R.D. was still at the pool hall.

She could almost hear Vik grumbling and complaining, hot like she was and ticked off at this waste of his Saturday afternoon. Vik liked to spend Saturdays with his grandkids, and she should be at Joanna's softball game.

A wind chime tinkled somewhere outside, a sharp sound like glass breaking. The wind must have been picking up, but there wasn't even a draft in the garage. She fanned herself with the girly magazine that had been shoved under the seat and took another sip of warm soda.

Earlier, after Mr. Martinez had left the precinct, she had gone upstairs to the squad room, still intending to finish a report and go to Joanna's game.

Vik had been sitting at his desk, wiry eyebrows clenched together. Behind him, through the wide expanse of windows in need of cleaning, the gray county buildings seemed to reflect the drab ill humor of the day.

The first thing she noticed as she walked into the squad room was how quiet it was. It was a brooding quiet—not the muffled hubbub of detectives at work, more like the storm gathering outside. Cowboy was leaning back in his chair, hat tilted back, the heels of his boots making new scars on the top of his desk. He was humming something tuneless, the way he always did when he was mad.

Slim was on the phone. "No, man," he almost hissed, his voice husky and compressed with annoyance. "Not the jail, dammit. Don't put me through to the jail again." He swore under his breath, drumming long tapered fingers on the departmental telephone directory. "Can somebody tell me what the hell's the use of putting in a new telephone system if the people you want to talk to aren't listed and you can't reach the ones who are because the phone that rings for their extension isn't anywhere near their desk?"

Slim sent his chair careening against the wall as he stood up. Marti caught the scent of Obsession as he went to the coffeepot. Usually he winked at her, and sometimes she winked back, but today his scowl was almost as fierce as Vik's. Everybody was in a lousy mood. She began to wonder what was wrong, then debated whether or not she wanted to find out. She flopped in her chair without speaking. There was a flagpole outside, and whenever there was a breeze a metal chain clanked against it. Today the sound was more annoying than usual.

She pulled out some forms, but before she could reach for a pen Vik tossed the weekend edition of the *News-Times* on her desk. She looked at the headline: CLINIC FIRE VICTIM IDENTIFIED.

She scanned the article. Nothing new. Same old information previously published. The headline was a question, not a statement. As usual, a source close to the investigation was certain they were close to a positive identification of the dead girl. Everyone must have read it, which explained their negative mood. The problem with this "source" was that nobody knew if somebody at the *News-Times* had made it up, guessed and gotten lucky every once in a while, or if someone in the department was leaking information.

As she stared at the headline, other implications began to occur to her. However unsubstantiated, this story was important to at least one person—whoever knew the girl while she was here, and whoever set the fire that killed her.

She tossed the paper back to Vik. "Anything to this?"

"Could be. Somebody in Louisiana or Kentucky somewhere has had a kid missing four, five weeks now. Just got around to reporting it."

"Didn't care." She spoke from experience. "Throwaway kids." She didn't understand it either.

"Could be our Jane Doe," Vik said. "Since you and our

local, friendly coroner are so buddy-buddy, maybe you could give her a call on it."

"Maybe." She put the blank report form back in her desk drawer. "What do we know about this girl who's been reported missing?"

"Thirteen. Black. Ran away."

"R.D." she said, recalling Isaac the Wino's singsong message. Little girls like little angels, ridin' 'round in birds with silver wings.

Vik rubbed his finger along the length of his beaked nose. "Figured you'd want to talk to R.D. We're working on locating him. Any good reason for thinking R.D.'s keeping baby dolls, other than not liking the man?"

"Informant."

"God help us. I suppose it's Cora, Queen of the Cockroaches this time. Or some other addlebrained half-wit."

She ignored his reference to Doretta Eldridge. "It was Isaac."

"Isaac the Wino? Has his brain suddenly remembered that it's supposed to record what he sees? Or are you basing this on something he heard while he was too drunk to understand what anyone was saying? If you think I'm going to rely on something Isaac thinks might have happened while he was having the DTs, you're as crazy as he is."

"We've got to assume R.D.'s read this. If he's got another little girl at his place he might want to get her out of there, might even risk taking her across the state line. Milwaukee, maybe. They've got a few meathouses for used-up child hookers."

"Not likely," Vik grumbled. "But what the hell. Guess maybe we should check out old R.D."

Vik usually didn't give up his Saturday afternoons that easily. Marti expected more of an argument. "Anything else I ought to know about this?" she said.

"No. Nothing wrong with hassling R.D."

She glanced at Slim, who gave her a thumbs-up sign. Damn.

If anything came of it, it would be their idea, not hers, and if nothing came of it, she'd be the butt of precinct jokes until something else came along worth laughing about.

A buzzing sound startled her. A wasp had landed on the side mirror. She debated rolling up the car window, decided it would be better to get stung than get heatstroke, and sat very still. The bug hovered a few inches above the hood, then veered and landed on the windshield wiper. As she slapped at the glass with the flat of her hand, a call came in on the car radio. R.D. was leaving the pool hall.

A few minutes later Linda came out of the house, exiting through the back door. Her hair had magenta streaks today. Linda looked around, opened the garage door, and went back into the house. When she emerged again, she had a young girl with her. The girl tried to pull away. Linda slapped her. Then, with one hand over the girl's mouth, she pushed her toward the garage.

16

In spiked heels Linda was almost a foot taller than the young girl. As soon as they went into the garage, Marti called in a description of the girl. "Black female, approximately five feet, weight eighty-five to ninety pounds." The clothing got her attention. It was similar to what the unidentified fire victim had been wearing when she died.

"Dressed like she's going to make her first Communion. White dress with lots of ruffles, white anklets, white patent leather shoes. Hair black or dark brown, short braids with white ribbons. Looks like R.D.'s got himself a baby doll. The child was resisting. She was slapped and pushed into the garage."

Within minutes, R.D. drove his gray Lincoln into the garage. Marti got a glimpse of his bodyguard Brick's bald head and massive shoulders as R.D. backed out again and drove away. Linda was in the backseat, and Marti could just see the top of the little girl's head through the rear window. As Marti watched, Linda pulled the girl down so that she couldn't be seen. She switched on her radio. "Minor sighted inside the vehicle. Request backup. Notify the sheriff's department."

She waited until Vik confirmed that R.D. had turned right on Second Avenue. They were heading for Route 41. A familiar tension gripped her shoulders as she leaned back against the seat. She preferred pursuits to stakeouts, and had to admit that she enjoyed a chase. But with a minor involved, they would have to be careful.

"Vik, you behind me?"

Vik confirmed. Slim and Cowboy fell in behind Vik, each in

a different vehicle. R.D. turned north on Route 41. They were about twenty-five miles south of the Wisconsin border. If they got lucky, R.D. would cross the state line.

R.D. kept his speed close to sixty. Marti slowed, allowed another car to pull in front of her. Slim and Cowboy switched to the left lane. Every time they came to an intersection she hunched forward, willing the Lincoln to continue north. When R.D. turned west on Route 173, she swore under her breath. An indirect route, maybe? Just a few more miles north and they'd be in Wisconsin. He might head north again.

When the car in front of her made a turn she decided to turn off too, make a right at the next stop sign, and let Vik pull up behind R.D. She made a U-turn, waited until Slim and Cowboy drove past, then pulled in behind them. They'd play tag like that for a while. Two county sheriff's units were pursuing along parallel routes.

Cowboy let a Jeep pull in front of him. Marti was five cars behind R.D. Once they had each taken a turn playing tag, a lot would depend on how often R.D. checked his rearview mirror and how observant he was when he did.

Brake lights flashed. R.D. turned right. They were just inside Antioch, not far from the state line. Maybe, she hoped. Another turn. Slim and Cowboy stopped just past a gravel driveway. She pulled in ahead of them and got out of her car as Vik parked farther ahead.

The driveway was curved and shaded with trees. She could see the peaked roof of a red brick house beyond it. Oaks grew to the north and south of the large lot, providing density and shade and isolating the house from its neighbors.

"Antioch," she said. "Damn."

"Yeah," Vik said. "We're still in Illinois."

The two sheriff's units pulled up. "Got a call in to the local force for assistance," the tallest sheriff's deputy said. "Too bad we can't nail him for transporting her across state lines."

When a local unit arrived they made their way along the

driveway, weapons drawn, using the trees to help them remain unobserved. R.D. had parked in front of the two-story house. Linda was still sitting in the backseat. She turned, saw them, didn't move. Marti motioned to one of the sheriff's deputies, who was armed with a rifle. Linda got out of the car and was cuffed without protest.

Marti motioned to the female deputy. "When we get inside, take care of the kid."

It was a large house, five bedrooms at least, Marti estimated. Red and white geraniums in cedarwood planters lined both sides of the steps leading to the front door. Marti tried the brass knocker. It was less intrusive than the bell.

A petite, dark-haired woman opened the door. "Damn it, Lin—"

Marti threw her weight against the door so the woman couldn't close it, grabbed her arm, and pulled her outside, holding her badge close to the woman's face.

"Peace officer, ma'am."

The woman gaped at her. "What?" She seemed stunned as Marti pushed her toward a deputy.

They entered the house, fanning out but moving toward the room where they heard voices.

". . . some kind of problem . . ."

"Problem!" R.D. yelled. "This little piece of shit . . ."

One of the local officers kicked open the door. "Peace officers. Don't move."

R.D. stood in the center of the room with a tall, slender blond man who seemed astonished to see them. Brick was sprawled on a couch with a placid expression on his tan face. Marti guessed his weight at 270. Taut muscles and huge biceps, no fat. The girl was sitting in a chair in the corner. Both windows were closed, but the room was pleasantly cool. Central air. The blond man took a step forward. "Now officers, I think . . ."

Cowboy trained his weapon on him. "Freeze or I'll shoot."

"But this is—"

"Home invasion, huh?" Slim sneered.

The girl began to whimper. Flat-chested and skinny, she didn't look more than ten or eleven. There were rope burns on her wrists, beginning to heal. The female deputy patted her down and took her into an adjoining room. Marti took a look around and, satisfied that things were under control, followed.

The room was filled with greenery: miniature orange and lemon trees, ferns, Swedish ivy, and dozens of African violets with pink and white flowers. The girl sat on the edge of a white wicker chair, gripping the thick green cushion with both hands. She stared at Marti's revolver.

"She's been advised of her rights," the deputy said and hurried out, eager to return to the action.

Marti holstered her weapon, watched as the girl began to relax a little, watched as a savvy, street-wise caution began to replace fear. This one had dealt with cops before. The rifles and semiautomatics were probably the only things unique to this arrest.

"You understand your rights?"

The girl's chin jutted out. She didn't release her tight grip on the cushions. Not sure of what was going to happen next. Pretty little girl. Not cute, but delicate. Dark eyes. Smooth, amber skin. Good bone structure. The kind of features that would keep her pretty well past middle age, if she lived that long. Marti felt her throat constrict, coughed, and read the girl her rights again, explaining them. "Want to tell me your name?"

"None ya business."

"Country," Momma would say, hearing that accent. The girl was from someplace in the South. It sounded like Louisiana.

"Baton Rouge?" Marti guessed.

"No." The surprised expression on her face told Marti that she was close. Some little town near there, most likely.

"You hear what they called you? A piece of shit. Meat. That all you wanna be, girl? Don't you think you're nothing more than that?"

The girl tilted her head at a defiant angle. "Worse things."

Marti looked at the rope burns, refused to let herself think about what worse things the girl could have experienced. "Suppose so," she agreed. "In your line of work."

Marti sat in one of the wicker chairs. "It would help to know your name. Save time if you just tell me so I don't have to take you in and run a make. I'd like to get you to the hospital, make sure you're okay."

"Check me for dope? I ain't doin' nothin' I can't do without."

She should have left this one to the state trooper. She hated getting involved with a kid who knew this much. "Your name?"

"Chrissie," the girl said.

"That what they call you?" Marti nodded toward the other room.

"So? What if they do?"

"What does your mother call you?"

The girl looked at the floor a minute, then looked at Marti again, defiant. "Where I lived they called me a narrow-assed hussy. You wanna call me that?"

"You like being called out of your name?" Marti persisted.

The girl looked away, not missing the implications of Marti's reference to naming, which was a personal, intimate experience among blacks. Nicknames were an insult unless they had a special meaning and were given with affection. Perhaps the significance of naming a child went back to slavery, when ancestral and historic names were arbitrarily replaced with Anglo, biblical, Christian names. Her children's names had been in their family for five generations.

"I can't call you Chrissie. What does your grandmother call you?"

The girl stared at the floor. "She dead. I'm named for her, though." She was silent again. Then, without looking up, she said, "Christina."

"Christina," Marti repeated. "I'm going to take you to the

hospital for observation. A juvenile officer and a social worker will interview you there."

Resignation. No interest. She'd been through this before.

"We'll notify your parents."

A smile. Bitter. Someone called a narrow-assed hussy at home probably had reasons for leaving. Marti stood up, feeling old, tired, wearied by this encounter with a child who shouldn't be this familiar with the system or this cynical. She hoped the girl's indifference was just pretense. "How old are you?"

"Twelve. The eighth of July."

Marti's stomach muscles tightened. "Time we got you out of here. I'll see you at the hospital, need to ask you some questions. Not that you have to answer." She went to the door and motioned for the state trooper to take Christina outside.

The blond guy with the little animal emblem on his polo shirt was being detained by one of the local cops. He kept glancing at the telephone, as if he was expecting it to ring. Most of the others were having a conference in the hall. Marti joined them.

"We don't have probable cause to search," a sheriff's deputy said.

"Shit," one of the Antioch cops complained. "We got a minor here, a known pimp. More than enough probable cause for a search if you ask me."

"We can't prove that the owners know anything about any of that."

"Called the state's attorney's office yet?" Marti asked, to cut the chitchat short.

Slim went to make the call, returned with a sour expression. "We couldn't talk them into nothing. Take the conservative approach. Arrest Linda, Brick, and R.D. Bring the homeowners in for questioning. You can always go back later. Damn."

Everyone including Marti was itching to take the place apart. Cowboy's nose was twitching. "Something's here," Marti said.

Vik grunted.

"Let's let Preppy's wife come back in," Marti suggested. "She might want to get her purse."

Grinning, Slim headed for the front door.

Marti accompanied the woman upstairs, down a long hall past four closed doors to the master bedroom. She noted two doors with padlocks. There was no drug paraphernalia or anything she could see that would justify a search. She had an untidy person's mistrust of anyone this orderly. The place didn't even look like anyone lived here. Mrs. Preppy went to a walk-in closet that was almost the size of Marti's bedroom. She got a pair of tennis shoes, took off her sandals, and placed them side by side where the tennis shoes had been. Her clothing hung along three walls, arranged by category.

Slim was waiting for them at the foot of the steps. "Could I please use your rest room?" he asked, smiling.

The woman seemed a bit taken aback, but nodded.

"Could I have some water, ma'am?" Vik asked.

"Sure."

This time Marti thought she detected a little sarcasm in the woman's voice.

"May I get it myself, ma'am?"

"Why not?"

Vik opened four cabinets before he looked in the one nearest the sink and found a glass. "Ice, ma'am?"

She shrugged.

He opened the refrigerator door. "Oops. Wrong side." He had the freezer door open before the woman could speak.

"The ice maker's on the door," she said.

"Oh, you've got one of those. Closest I've ever been to one." He gulped down the water without waiting for it to get cold.

Slim came to the kitchen door and shook his head. Nothing incriminating in any of the bathrooms, either. Disappointed, they headed for their cars.

17

From Antioch, Marti and Vik drove back to Lincoln Prairie and went to R.D.'s house. Because Marti had observed Christina being taken forcibly from the house to the garage, the lieutenant had been able to obtain a search warrant.

It was almost six o'clock when they pulled up in front of the beige and brick two-story house. Two patrol cars were parked outside. As Marti got out of the Chevy, a pleasant breeze blew against her arms and her face. It was getting cooler, and the day's mugginess was gone. She surveyed the yard: close-cropped grass, no flowers, high, dense hedges and fir trees that provided privacy on three sides but left the back of the house exposed.

"Anybody home?" she asked the uniform who opened the door.

"Just one young lady by the name of Glodine," the middle-aged, bespectacled uniform told her. "Glodine says she had surgery about three weeks ago. She's here recuperating."

There were footsteps and banging noises upstairs. The toss was still going down. The uniform pointed to a room to Marti's right and stayed near the front door.

The place wasn't what she expected. Cozy was a good way to describe it. Floor-to-ceiling maple paneling, chintz curtains, early American furniture in golds and browns. Milk-glass lamps with ruffled shades. A fireplace, and on the wall above the mantel, a large brass eagle with outstretched wings. Norman Rockwell prints on the other walls. Glodine was sitting in a thickly upholstered rocker. Marti told the uniform standing beside the chair to join Vik in the hallway.

Glodine gave her a disinterested glance, then looked away. She was wearing a loose-fitting shift, and there was a glossy shine on her face. A facial, Marti decided, one of those made of egg whites or something that dried like a thin layer of skin. They must have interrupted her when they came to toss the place, without letting her rinse it off. It looked dry and uncomfortable now.

"I don't suppose you know anything about Christina?"

"Don't know nothin'," Glodine said.

"She was observed leaving this house this afternoon."

"Wouldn't know."

"Weren't you home?"

"Been sick. In bed mostly."

Glodine looked as if she was recovering from a beating, but said she had fallen down a flight of stairs. She gave her age as nineteen. No use asking what Glodine had done to earn a beating, but it might be interesting to know. According to Cowboy and Slim, R.D. had a reputation for treating his women pretty well.

"You do not know of any minor child leaving this residence this afternoon?"

"Sure don't. Why? Is that what everyone's here lookin' for?"

"We have her in custody."

Marti waited in vain for Glodine to react. If Christina had any friends here, Glodine sure wasn't one of them. It didn't look as if she gave a damn about anybody other than herself.

Glodine rubbed at her face. "Mind if I go upstairs and wash this off? It's itching."

Marti nodded, curious to see the rest of the place, and escorted her out of the room.

Vik raised his eyebrows as she passed. Marti blinked twice. No. She didn't want him along.

They passed a half bath. Marti wondered why Glodine didn't go in there, but she didn't insist. The woman was up to something.

The upstairs rooms were a shambles. Clothing was tossed everywhere. Furniture had been pulled away from the walls. Bureau drawers and their contents were dumped on the floor. Footsteps overhead indicated that the search had progressed to the attic. Marti hoped they had found something—drugs, drug paraphernalia, anything that would incriminate R.D. and be enough to get him tried and convicted.

"I need to get something out of one of the rooms. That okay?"

Marti started to say no, then wondered why Glodine had said one of the rooms and not "my room."

"Don't take long."

"Just be a minute."

Glodine kicked clothing out of her way as she walked down the hall, then stopped.

"Your room?" Marti asked.

"Yeah."

"What a mess."

Glodine shrugged. Too detached, Marti decided. Didn't care about Christina, didn't care about her room getting tossed. Much too calm.

"Got a bathroom in here."

The room they entered was small. A single bed, a three-drawer bureau, and little mess. Feminine. Pink ruffled curtains, matching bedspread. There wasn't much to toss, just bed linens and a few pieces of jewelry scattered on shaggy pink carpeting.

"Junk," Glodine said, kicking at a necklace. "Don't even know who it belongs to. Ain't never even seen none of this stuff before. Bathroom's right here." Marti went in with her and watched as she rinsed off the facial.

As Glodine came out of the bathroom she lurched against

the wall, as if she had a cramp in her leg. She took another step, then grabbed at her ankle. "Ouch." She pressed her weight on the foot for a minute, then reached down, rubbing her instep.

When she stood up, Marti noticed that a ring she had seen on the rug was no longer there.

"Want to give me that ring, Glodine?"

"What you talkin' 'bout?"

It was an unconvincing bluff. "Just give it to me. Now."

Glodine looked past her, as if she wished she could walk out of the room, then complied.

The ring was made of tin, and small enough to fit Marti's pinkie—or a child's finger. A small, red glass stone was flanked by two clear glass chips. Marti called for the recording officer, then asked for whoever had searched the room. A leggy red-haired young woman came down from the attic. Marti had seen her at the precinct but didn't know her by name yet. "You search this room?"

"Yes, ma'am."

"Take a look around. Is anything missing that was here when you searched?"

"Nothing much in here," the uniform remarked. "Some costume jewelry in the left top drawer."

Marti said nothing, waiting.

The uniform looked down. "A ring. It was on the rug. Can't remember what it looked like. Red. Something red."

Marti showed her the ring, and she identified it. Satisfied that a chain of evidence had been established, Marti gave the ring to the recording officer.

She took another look around. A clean room with one bed. No roaches, rats, or bedbugs. A bathroom where you could take a bath or a shower, a lot better than a public facility where you could just wash your face and hands. A place like this could seem like a palace to a kid on the street, and she might be willing to do a lot of things to stay here.

Marti went into the hall, with Glodine and the two officers following her. Turning, she glimpsed an expression on Glodine's face that she could only describe as satisfaction. Had Glodine wanted to hide the ring, or call attention to it?

18

When Marti and Vik returned to the precinct, R.D. was waiting for them in the interrogation room. Just as in the past, he did not want an attorney to represent him.

"Arrogant bastard," Vik said. "Gets away with so much he thinks he can do anything he wants. He didn't have a chance to talk this one over with Brick. I don't think he realizes what we've got this time."

"I want him," Marti said as she pushed open the door.

R.D. was sitting at the round wooden table. He glanced at Vik and stared at Marti, his expression intense, as if he was trying to intimidate her. There was a boyishness to his dark, round face, the roundness exaggerated by his close-cut kinky-black hair. Conservative in a dark pinstriped suit with a mauve shirt and gray tie, R.D. didn't have the clothes or the mannerisms stereotypical of a pimp. Under different circumstances Marti could have mistaken him for a legitimate businessman.

He leaned back, arms folded, looking at her in much the same way that a prizefighter might stare down his opponent. She took a chair and straddled it.

"Paperwork in order?" she asked Vik. It was idle conversation. She wasn't ready to give R.D. her full attention. She didn't want to talk to R.D. tonight, she wanted to whip up on him. Child procurer. Child molester. Cradle-robbing bastard. What in hell could a grown man want with a child that age, a child that small and physically immature? The muscles in her neck and shoulders tensed. In half an hour she'd be aching from not hitting him.

The door opened. Marti smelled Obsession and looked up. Slim gave her a quick smile and sat down. His nonchalant attitude made him seem imperturbable, but Marti knew how angry he was and wondered if R.D. could tell.

Cowboy came in behind Slim and leaned against the cinder-block wall. His jaw was puffed out with a wad of chewing gum. The muscles in his arms and shoulders seemed taut.

Distracted, R.D. looked from one of them to the other. Marti stared at him until he was looking at her. "I just put a call in to the hospital. You've been having a lot of fun with Christina."

"That's what you say. Ain't got no proof of nothing. You ain't never had no proof, ain't never gonna get no proof. If I were you, I'd just leave me alone."

"Wouldn't have thought your taste ran to children." She kept her voice low and calm. "Department shrink says men who like 'em that young got problems, that you're afraid to deal with a real woman because you're not sure if you're a real man."

R.D.'s hand was flat on the table. She watched as his fingers curled into a fist.

"That why you got to have women hustling for you, make you feel like a man? Something going on with you that makes you scared to deal with a woman you can't sell, something that's bad enough to get you running to little girls to feel big and strong?"

R.D. kept looking at her. There was a slight twitch at the corner of his left eye. Except for that, his face remained impassive. He clenched his fist a little tighter.

"Where are your two daughters?" she asked. "Texas someplace? Kept your old lady on her back while she was pregnant with both of 'em, didn't you? Sure they're yours? That your problem, R.D.? Shootin' blanks? Or *are* they your kids? That why she left you, to keep you from selling your own kids? Or from sleeping with 'em? That what you got on your mind when you're humpin' Christina, those two little girls down in Texas? Be what, eleven and twelve now? Must need something small, cause I bet you ain't got enough to satisfy something adult-sized."

The tic at the corner of R.D.'s eye jerked faster. People like him made Marti debate the pros and cons of being charged with police brutality. Vik was breathing with deep nasal snorts, and Cowboy was cracking his knuckles. Slim, studiously impassive, looked dangerous.

"Got some real problems with it, huh, R.D.?"

Sweat was beginning to bead on R.D.'s upper lip. His forehead was glistening. Marti thought about the ring she had found at his house. She didn't think it was something a man like him would notice, and decided not to show it to him.

"Shrink says little girls seem safe to a man having trouble getting it up or coming too fast. Premature ejaculation. Hard for a grown woman to pretend she likes that. Little kids are glad to get it over with. Damned shame, man, not having what it takes to satisfy a woman. They laugh at you when you show it to 'em?"

R.D.'s eye was twitching so hard it was pulling at the whole side of his face. "You got me in here to question me. You signifying b—"

"Uh-uh, man," Slim cautioned. "Big Mac here don't take to being called outta her name. She's being real friendly right now. You don't want her to get mad."

"You got any questions for me?" R.D. demanded.

Slim decided he needed an interpreter. "You got any questions for him, Mac?"

She shook her head, spoke to Slim. "Just making conversation."

Cowboy inspected the heel of his boot. "Heavy shit, man. Got you charged with kidnapping, rape, procurement."

R.D. leaned forward. "Don't touch no kids."

"Oh, come on!" Slim scoffed. "With your problems? Cute little kid like that. She looks something like your kids, maybe."

"Don't mess with no kids," R.D. repeated, louder.

"Best hold it down," Slim advised. "Keep cool. Big Mac

here's having a tough time staying friendly tonight. I don't think you want to run up against no real woman, R.D."

"Be best if you stick with little kids," Cowboy agreed. "Most likely they're about as much as you can handle."

R.D. slammed his fist on the table. His face contorted. "I told you, man. I don't do that." He looked at her. "You started this shit. You . . . you—"

"Keep your voice down," Slim said. "You're in enough trouble. You don't want to be charged with threatening a peace officer."

R.D. started to get up. Marti shifted in her chair and he sat back, rapping his fist on the table. "I'll be a son of a bitch," he muttered.

"You said it." She smiled, getting up. "Oh, and watch your back. You know how it is when word gets 'round a jail that you play with children. Real men tend to dislike people like that. Could get rough for you in there."

R.D. looked from one of them to the other. He looked at Marti last. "Shit," he said as she walked out of the room.

In the corridor, Slim winked at her. "One pimp adequately deballed," he said.

Vik scowled, annoyed by the comment. "Does her job," was all he said.

Cowboy patted her on the shoulder. She braced herself as soon as she saw it coming and didn't wince as he thumped her with one hard whack.

She spoke to Slim. "Linda's next. Nice of her to refuse to have a lawyer present."

"Stupid," Slim said. "Both of them. I hope none of the 'jailhouse lawyers' in there clue them in."

"What do I need to know about her?" She didn't know Linda at all, except by sight.

"Likes an audience. Real cute little actress when she gets some attention."

"So I'll see her alone. Sit on the other side of the two-way mirror."

"Oh, and there's Annie Lewis, one of our local, friendly hookers," Slim added. "She and Linda hate each other's guts. But Annie's bigger. Beat Linda's ass one night. Linda don't like nothing physical. Probably why she's with R.D. Her momma used to give her them down-home whippings that made you wish you'd never been born. I've been savin' that one, Mac. You owe me." He gave her a dimpled grin that failed to make her heart melt.

"I owe you," she said, opening the door to the interrogation room.

She sat across the table from Linda. This close, Linda's magenta-streaked hair looked stiff as straw. Purple and red shadow was smeared on the woman's eyelids and her fingernails were painted a matching shade. The red metallic threads woven through her skimpy black stretch top did little more than emphasize the smallness of her breasts.

The room was cool. Marti wondered if Linda was cold but didn't ask. The girl was so skinny she looked like a thirteen-year-old anorexic.

Linda spoke first. "So what you want with me, Miss Officer? I never even got outta the car."

"You know what you're charged with?"

"I ain't aided and abetted nothin'. Ain't been no kind of accomplice. Ain't done nothin' lately but sell a little ass and ain't even done that today."

Listening to her, Marti realized this was what it could be like talking to Christina in another year or two. Linda was only eighteen. With R.D. she had an easy life as a hooker's life goes, but she looked old—brittle and old and used. The expression in her eyes was dull, as if there wasn't much that interested her anymore. And the drugs she was taking were eating away at her.

"What are you on? Besides heroin."

"You worried 'bout me, Miss Officer?" Linda sneered.

"Waste of time. I've gone cold turkey before. Do it again if I gotta."

Marti felt tired, too tired to do what she considered necessary now. She leaned back a little and smiled. Best to get it over with and go home. "Friend of yours'll be joining you tonight. Annie Lewis."

Linda looked like she was going to be sick.

"Hear you two are real tight."

"What you want?" Linda's voice was hoarse.

"Don't want nothing, not a thing."

Linda looked scared to death.

"I asked them to put Annie in the cell next to yours. Guess you'll be real glad to see her. Nice having a friend that close when you're locked up in a place like this."

Marti stood up. She pulled out the ring she had found at R.D.'s and let it drop on the table.

Linda jumped up. "Bathroom," she gasped, clapping her hand over her mouth.

Marti just stood there.

"Bathroom, please."

Marti called the guard after Linda began retching. This would not endear Linda to the sheriff's deputies who staffed the jail. Time to go home. Vik could take care of Brick. She felt tired as hell.

It was raining as Marti drove home. She parked in the driveway and listened to the rain beating against the car in rhythms that would put her to sleep if she sat there long enough. The house was dark and quiet. She had hoped to make it home before the party was over. Joanna was sure to have mustered enough enthusiasm to have a good time. It was hard to imagine Joanna being shy. She rotated her neck to ease the stiffness. God, she was tired. It had been a long day, and she had just come from seeing Christina at the hospital, but she wasn't going to think about that tonight.

Thunder crackled, and she counted to three before lightning leaped down in jagged blue-white streaks. She liked storms. "Lord's cleaning the world," Momma would say, watching from the window as the rain ran in wide rivers along the curb. "Makin' all things new."

"He's sure gotta do it often enough," she would answer. "Could just keep it raining all the time around here."

Storms had seemed so far away in the city, high above the tall buildings, more noisy than powerful. Here there were times when she thought she could reach out and grab hold of the lightning.

The rhythm of the rain began to soothe her as she looked out at the dark sky. She began to relax. They had put in a good day's work. R.D., Linda, and Brick were in jail. Linda was in a cell next to Annie. That girl sure had been scared. How had Glodine's beating affected her? Was she scared about that too, afraid that she might be next? At least Christina was safe, for now. She wouldn't be turning tricks, not for a while.

The Antioch couple were being held overnight. Calm and self-assured, they had refused to speak with anyone but their attorney, a Chicago lawyer with a LaSalle Street address, big money. The state's attorney's office had decided that a search of their house was in order, and that it was reasonable to detain them for twenty-four hours.

She smiled. She would question them in the morning. By then they would have an idea of what life in prison could be like.

She thought of the anonymous caller who had fingered R.D. for the clinic torching. Then she thought of the ring she had turned in as evidence. Who did it belong to? Christina had denied that it was hers.

19

Marti left the house Sunday morning a little before eight. Church services didn't begin until eleven, and everyone else was still asleep. The sky was a clear, cloudless blue, the day already warm. A few tree boughs littered the street, a reminder of the thunderstorm the night before.

Last night she had driven to the hospital to see Christina. There was a Catholic hospital on the other side of town, but most police cases were brought here and she was familiar with the layout of each wing. Rain had splattered against her slicker as she sprinted for the double doors. She bypassed the emergency room and negotiated a mazelike series of turns that took her into the north wing. Christina was in the adolescent chemical dependency unit, a locked ward with watchful nurses and attendants. An aide directed her to a room at the far end of the hall.

"How's the patient?" she asked.

"Just fine, so far. Quiet. Hasn't gone down to the rec room."

"Juvenile officer been here yet?"

"Yeah. Didn't stay long."

"Know who it was?"

"Denise Stevens."

"Good." Denise was a no-nonsense woman with a lot of experience. She did as much as she could for the kids assigned to her. Marti went down the hall, pausing just outside Christina's room. The door was open. Patients weren't allowed to close them.

It was a small room, two beds, both with green spreads pulled taut. Green-white-and-yellow-striped curtains hung at the window, and a helium-filled balloon that said WE CARE was tied to the back of the chair, a welcome from the staff.

Christina was standing by the window, arms folded, looking out at the gathering storm. She turned as Marti entered the room, looked at her for a minute with dark solemn eyes, but said nothing.

Marti walked closer. "Like storms?"

The girl shrugged. She was wearing a green hospital gown and had plaited her hair in two cornrows that made her look even younger than twelve.

"When I was a kid my mother would make us unplug everything during a storm and sit in the dark in the middle bedroom, the one with no windows. Then she'd tell us stories from the Bible."

Christina didn't respond. "Do you need anything?" Marti asked.

"Other lady asked me that. Don't need nothin'."

Marti looked at the rope burns on the girl's wrists. She had seen a lot of abused children in Chicago. Children who were horribly beaten. Children who were disfigured. Children who were dead. At least Christina was still alive. "A girl about your age died here in a fire a couple weeks ago."

"So?"

"We don't know who she was, where she came from. Runaway, most likely. Fire happened at a clinic. Haven't heard nothing about it, have you?"

"Nothin' to me. Wouldn't know."

"Someone set the fire. Killed her and another girl. You think of something you might have overheard . . ."

Christina turned to her. "Said I don't know nothin'. It legal, you comin' here botherin' me?"

The aide came in then with apple juice and graham crackers. Marti left. The aide knew more about handling disturbed adolescents than she did. Dealing with juveniles depressed her, took something she didn't have. No way she could balance her own inability to see that the kids got what they needed—parents, home, or whatever—with the reality of foster care and detention halls and what too many of the kids would become.

Marti looked out at the bright morning sunlight, and checked her watch. It was only 8:15. She pulled into a fast-food place and sat in the parking area, drinking coffee and eating the breakfast special. Joanna called it a cholesterol sandwich. Marti wondered how the party had gone last night.

20

As soon as Marti got to the pre-
cinct she grabbed a second cup of coffee and went over to her
desk. Vik sat across from her, scowling as usual. Church services
always put her in a good mood, but Sunday Mass never seemed
to have a similar effect on Vik. She didn't think his expression
had changed once since Friday.

"If you don't stop frowning so much, Vik, your eyebrows
are going to get all tangled up and start growing across the
bridge of your nose."

He grunted.

"And my mother always says that if you keep your mouth
all puckered up like that your lips will get stuck one day and
you'd have to talk like this for the rest of your life." She said
"Good morning" with her lips pursed the way his were.

Vik didn't smile, but the corners of his mouth turned up
just a little. "I don't know what's got you in such a good mood,
MacAlister. Wait'll you see this report."

"Now what?"

"State Drug Enforcement. They found half a pound of cocaine at the Antioch house. Cost about sixteen thousand, worth
about a hundred thousand on the street."

She whistled. "Class X felony, six to twenty. Damn."

"And," Vik went on, "they also found a lot of kiddy porn
and filming equipment. Ties in with a state investigation, so
we've lost out on that part of the case, too. We don't even get an
honorable mention for the raid that stirred things up."

"And the lieutenant's unhappy."

"I suggested that he take his complaint to the state's attorney's office. We just followed their orders."

"And missed out on a major drug bust." If there hadn't been three different law enforcement agencies involved when they got to that house, Marti would have come up with the justification and made a field decision to turn that place upside down.

"Damn search-and-seizure laws," Vik complained.

He had been a cop before the most recent statutes were written. When Marti came on the force she had learned ways to circumvent them without doing anything illegal. Not that she minded having those laws. People had a right to that kind of protection, and cops needed that kind of leash sometimes.

"Did the state release any information to us on their investigation?"

"Have they ever?"

"Who'd you talk to?"

"Nobody. They faxed this report, which says nothing, and I got a five-minute lecture from the lieutenant about thinking on your feet."

"Let me see the report."

She read through three pages of double-talk. The Antioch couple hadn't even been under surveillance, but the state was aware of illicit drug, prostitution, and child pornography activity in the Lake County area. The R.D. bust involving Christina must have tipped off the state cops. She hadn't even gotten a chance to question Preppy and his wife, and now it was too late.

She scanned the report again. Not one state investigator's name, nobody identified whom she could talk to. "This is so clean we could publish it in the *News-Times* and nobody would bother to read it."

Marti loved the way one law enforcement agency kept secrets from another. Officially it was called security, but she thought it was just another way of giving the local force the middle finger. "Politics," she muttered under her breath. "Damn."

Vik took the report, made a motion as if he were going to toss it into the wastebasket, threw it on his desk instead. "Damn," he agreed. "Maybe the Feds will confiscate their property. Nobody's even talking about the kiddie porn. Yet. The drug bust is too big."

"The worst thing about kiddie porn is that the photographs are used to recruit children into that kind of activity," Marti said. She shuddered, thinking about it.

"Never could work Vice," Vik said.

She left him sitting there shaking his head and headed to the southwest suburbs, where Dr. Edwards and his wife lived. Arborview Oaks was a subdivision about twenty miles west of Lincoln Prairie. She chose a route with several farms sprawled on either side of a two-lane road. Cornstalks stood tall, and alfalfa swayed in green ripples. She turned off the air conditioning and rolled down the window, enjoying the warm breeze that blew on her face and the smell of moist earth and growing things that seemed more intense after last night's heavy rain.

Arborview Oaks was a new development, very expensive and exclusive, and it wouldn't surprise her if the Edwardses were the only blacks who lived there. She thought of it as one of those developments designed for the recently wealthy who were still becoming accustomed to their new social status and investment portfolios. Buyers chose from three or four basic models and made enough alterations for their houses to look different from the others without creating any significant variations. Their belief in their own uniqueness remained intact without giving them any anxiety about not being just like everyone else.

She equated developments like this with the "ticky tackys" described in the song years ago. If she could afford a place like this, she'd find a house built with old money that had a little class.

The doctor's house was a sprawling brick tri-level set on a

large lot. An attached three-car garage made it seem slightly different from the nearest neighbors, but Marti was certain the floor plans were the same. Sod had been laid and four saplings were anchored in place with rubber collars and taut wires. A white Jaguar and a black Bentley were parked in the driveway.

A slender woman of medium height opened the door. "Oh, I was expecting. . . ." she began, then said, "Jane Law, how nice." Her tone of voice and the expression on her face suggested the sudden awareness of rotting fish. "I was hoping that business at my husband's clinic could be kept away from my home." She looked around as if she was concerned with which of the neighbors might be watching.

"Perhaps I could come in," Marti suggested.

A car went by, and Mrs. Edwards opened the door just wide enough to let Marti squeeze in.

"I just need to ask you a couple of questions."

"And I suppose you were just in the neighborhood and thought you'd stop by."

The foyer was large but Mrs. Edwards hadn't moved more than a foot from the door. Marti felt the spiny leaves of a plant against her arm. She didn't like feeling cornered, so she took a step sideways, then a step forward until Mrs. Edwards backed away, brushing at her beige silk blouse as if she had gotten too close to something that would soil it. The blouse and the taupe slacks Mrs. Edwards was wearing reminded Marti of the clothes on a mannequin she had seen as she was taking a shortcut through Carson, Pirie, Scott on her way to Sears.

Mrs. Edwards was a little too tall to be considered petite. Her light brown hair was clipped in a short, pixielike style. Her eyes were hazel, the tilt of her nose pert. She could pass for white if she wanted to, her skin was so light.

"I suppose now that you're here you'd like to come in and take a look around." She turned abruptly, and Marti followed her into the living room. The first thing she thought of was a class trip to the Art Institute when she was in grade school. It took her a minute to figure it out. The room measured at least forty-five by thirty feet and everything was white—walls, carpet, drapes, lacquered tables. She headed for the built-in cabinets between the windows.

Mrs. Edwards stepped in front of her, checking to see that the glass doors were locked. Marti noticed some tiny pry marks that marred the wood and looked fresh. She'd check for a police report.

"Dresden," Mrs. Edwards said with obvious pride, pointing to several cups and saucers. "Antique," she explained. "Eighteen-fifty."

She pointed out a crystal inkwell, then a bowl, mentioned names and dates. A careful collection of small items, nothing that struck Marti as unusual, assembled by someone who wanted each item to be correct. Candlesticks, paperweights, a few figurines, nothing that interested her.

Turning, she noticed a pewter tankard on a table and picked it up. It wasn't as heavy as it looked.

"Sherman Boardman," Mrs. Edwards said, taking a step closer. "Eighteen-fifty-one. Picked it up last week. I haven't decided to keep it, though."

Marti wondered if it was an impulse purchase that hadn't been checked out with the decorator yet.

"I suppose you've come to ask me about James's financial records?" Mrs. Edwards said.

"I understand you're trying to piece together some information for us, reconstruct some of the financial documents that were destroyed."

"Yes. Of course, that will take time. I have other responsibilities. I just returned from a business trip to Washington, D.C., and I have some very important social commitments in the next few weeks."

"I understand."

"Good of you to be so patient."

"Oh, I'm not," Marti told her, sensing that Mrs. Edwards

was becoming suspicious of her apparent good nature. "I just have other things to be concerned with. We don't know the identity of one of the girls who died in the fire, and then there's the arsonist. I'm sure we won't find anything out of order with whatever information you provide."

Mrs. Edwards came as close to smiling as she was likely to do. She could reconstruct her husband's financial data into whatever would conform with IRS and other public records. If there were any discrepancies between that and the data contained on the diskettes, there would be no way to prove it. Marti hoped that Mrs. Edwards would be so confident of her ability to get away with this that she wouldn't destroy the copies of the correct information that she must still have.

The tour began and ended with the living room. There was not one personal item to indicate that anyone but the decorator took any interest in the place. Even the collectibles could have been assembled by someone paid to do that.

As she reached the door, Mrs. Edwards said, "Sometimes you people really surprise me."

Marti hated the term *you people.*

"On the one hand you complain because blacks at our level don't help the poor. Then, when James goes back to provide medical services in a place like that instead of building his practice among the wealthy, you people persecute him because someone burns down his clinic." Mrs. Edwards stood with her hands on her hips, as emotional as Marti had seen her—not very, but emphatic. "James comes from a large family. He has four brothers and six sisters, and God knows how many nieces and nephews. He feels a responsibility to see that those women have access to abortions and contraceptives. My God, if they don't stop multiplying like rabbits . . . the welfare system is strangling us now. Do you have any idea of how much it costs us when these children are born? Or the resources that wanted children are deprived of? You of all people should appreciate what James does. You're the one who will arrest the thieves and prostitutes and drug addicts they'll become."

Marti didn't respond, but she wondered why Mrs. Edwards believed that all children born to the poor were unwanted. Was she thinking of her own family as she spoke? Then she wondered what Dr. Edwards's attitude toward his patients, which seemed to her one of collective concern but individual indifference, said about his upbringing as one of many children.

One thing was certain, those services Dr. Edwards was so generously providing to keep welfare payments down kept Medicare and Medicaid costs up. To judge by his house and his cars, this gift of his services to "those people" in "a place like that" paid well.

21

It was a little before one o'clock, sunny, and hot as Marti turned onto Route 41 and headed south toward Chicago. She popped one of Johnny's tapes into the cassette player. Johnny had collected recordings from the fifties. He had more than seven hundred LPs, forty-fives, and old seventy-eights recorded on tape. She kept a few cassettes with fast, up-tempo songs in the car. She had a few with slow, sentimental tunes in her room. The original records and albums were stored in a cool place in the basement. Now she sang along to a Shirley and Lee song, "I Feel Good."

She remembered Johnny's baritone. It was a gentle kind of memory, comforting. She liked thinking of him that way, singing and having a good time, not worrying about the job, not concerned with drug deals or weapons, just feeling good.

Instead of exiting at Roosevelt Road and heading west to the Pilsen area, she stayed on the expressway until she reached Garfield Boulevard. She switched off the tape and rolled down the window, felt the heat oozing in. Noise seemed to roll in, too—traffic sounds, a radio blaring, an argument.

She took the curving road that cut through the park and passed the DuSable Museum. This was the scenic route that went past her old house. Their house. Hers and Johnny's.

A teenager on roller blades was gliding along beside the car on the passenger side, eyeing Marti's purse on the seat. She flashed her shield and he moved on, giving her a military salute.

"Ambience," Johnny would have teased, tossing off a oneworder the way comics toss off one-liners. She would have laughed.

She drove past the house slowly. Pale green siding, two stories plus cellar and attic. It was squeezed onto the smallest plot of land possible, two feet on either side and about four feet of grass front and back. Johnny's irises were gone, replaced with marigolds. Thank God she had taken some of the rhizomes with her when she'd left. She shouldn't have come here. It wasn't their house anymore.

She took Cottage Grove back to Roosevelt and drove west to Ashland, thinking about Carmen Rodriguez, the doctor's other evening receptionist. Carmen had come to Chicago to stay with her grandmother immediately after Teresa's funeral. When she had questioned the young woman the day after the fire, Carmen hadn't told her anything that differed from what the doctor said.

Marti had spoken with Carmen's two older sisters. According to them, Carmen was thoughtless and inconsiderate. She also resented having to send part of her wages to her parents and stayed out until all hours with her boyfriend. Carmen was lazy, did not help out at home, and spent too much on clothing and cosmetics.

Marti had no clear impression of the girl, but her sisters were unanimous in their opinion of her. Now, even though Carmen hadn't been at the clinic the night of the fire, Marti wanted to talk with her again.

The address was a wood-framed two-flat. An old woman answered the door. At first she spoke in Spanish, but when Marti pretended not to understand she switched to a pidgin English.

"Who you want here?"

"You're Carmen's grandmother?"

"Sí."

"Is she at home?"

Instead of replying, the woman examined Marti's shield, holding it close to dark, watery eyes. "Carmencita?" she said.

Marti decided to speak Spanish, not fluently, which she could do, but in the halting syllables of someone with a limited vocabulary. *"Donde está,* Carmen?" No need to let the old woman know she understood too much of the language.

A five-minute bartering session ensued, mostly in English. When the grandmother determined to her satisfaction that Marti was indeed a peace officer, that this was an unofficial visit, that it shouldn't take longer than fifteen minutes and her granddaughter wouldn't be arrested, Marti was allowed to enter the flat.

The apartment smelled of tortillas and homemade beef and chicken fillings for burritos and chimichangas—smells that could have lingered in these walls for thirty years. Just walking through the door made Marti feel hungry.

Carmen was sitting on a lumpy sofa that looked old enough to be stuffed with horsehair. Her legs were tucked under her and she was reading a paperback, *Wuthering Heights.* Her dark hair had swung forward, partially shielding her face, but Marti could see she wasn't wearing any makeup. An unblemished complexion, long eyelashes, and a shy, tentative smile made cosmetics unnecessary.

Marti sat across from Carmen in a chair that was hard and uncomfortable. The grandmother stood in the doorway, scuffing one felt slipper against worn linoleum. The old woman's hair was thick, more yellow than white, and coiled at the nape of her neck. Those dark eyes would miss nothing.

She looked about the room. A small statue of the Virgin of Guadalupe sat on the mantel. Braided rugs made of bright red, yellow, blue, and green rags tossed on the linoleum. The floor was warped and slanted down toward the sofa.

"You want to ask me more questions, Detective MacAlister?" Carmen asked. "I don't remember what you asked me the last time."

Marti considered what she needed to find out. "Why are you here and not working?"

"The doctor says there will be no evening clinic for a while. He thinks I should come here. He paid me for another six weeks even though I am not there."

"Why does he pay you and Teresa so much money?"

Carmen seemed startled by her question. "He says it is not a nice neighborhood, that I stay too late at night and there are no buses running when I go home."

Speaking in Spanish, the grandmother said, "What do your sisters know?"

Carmen looked at Marti. "You have not told my sisters that he pays me twelve-fifty an hour? They think it is only four twenty-five."

"No." The deception didn't surprise her, but the amount he was paying her did. One or both of the girls had to be assisting him with more than routine office work. "Why was Teresa working the night of the fire?"

"The doctor said he wanted her there."

"What were you doing that night?"

Carmen began fidgeting with the pages of the paperback.

"Were you with your boyfriend?"

Carmen looked down. "I was at the library, studying. You will not tell?"

Marti wasn't sure why something like that should be kept a secret. "How did you get this job with the doctor?"

"Teresa. She worked there. She didn't want to work all of the nights, though. So I went in her place."

Dr. Edwards had said he hired Carmen, not Teresa. That Carmen answered an ad. "Did you and Teresa have a work schedule?"

Carmen shook her head.

"How did you know when you'd work?"

"Teresa works when the doctor asks her to. The other nights it's me. She calls to let me know."

"Was there any particular time when Teresa always worked?"

Carmen wound a strand of hair around her finger. A plump, tiger-striped cat came in, brushing against the cotton stockings that covered the old woman's legs, greeting her with a muted meow. "You should tell her," the woman said. "She does not bring harm."

Carmen released the strand of hair. "There was something different about the nights that Teresa was there. I am not sure what. He taught Teresa to assist him. When I am there I do not go into the examining room with him. Teresa did. Dr. Edwards does not do anything wrong. If you are young, and your period is just a little late, sometimes he will help you. There are some he tells he cannot help. He is. . . ." She groped for words. "He is not unkind. He likes me, I think. He does not speak often, so it is hard to know. One night I was wearing my hair tied with a ribbon. It came undone and he tied it, like a father would. His hands are gentle. He does not want anything from me."

"Tell her you do not want her to say this to anyone else," the old woman urged.

Carmen repeated that in English.

"I can't promise that you will never be called to testify in court, but I don't think so."

Before she left, Marti accepted a glass of lemonade and gave Carmen the name of a social worker she knew who would be able to help her get job training or financial assistance for college.

22

Early Monday morning Marti drove over to see Doretta Eldridge. When Doretta had called the night before she had seemed more annoyed than anxious, and Marti decided that whatever it was could wait until she got a decent night's sleep. Doretta was an early riser and more preoccupied with housework than religion at this time of day. There wouldn't be any sermons.

Marti left the house without having breakfast. She stopped at a bakery and bought a dozen sweet rolls. It was a few minutes past seven when she got to the Eldridge residence, unlatched the gate, and took a narrow concrete path to the rear of the house. The back porch was winterized, and an elderly washing machine installed there was wheezing through the spin cycle. Two more loads of clothes were sorted and waiting. She tapped on the door.

In a minute Doretta was looking at her with a nearsighted squint. Her dark, angular face was shiny with sweat, and she wiped her hands on a bib apron worn over a cotton housedress. "Why Sister MacAlister, so good to see you. So nice of you to come right away. The night watchman turneth away and the horsemen come trampling down the harvest."

Marti followed Doretta into the boxlike kitchen with the blue tile floor and glossy white walls. Doretta went to a pot simmering on a stove so old it had feet.

"I'm making some applesauce for Poppa." She lifted the lid and the aroma of fruit and cinnamon was sweet and strong. "Apples. Poppa's favorite," Doretta said. " 'Fraid he'd choke though, if they wasn't cooked. Can't hardly chew no more since his stroke."

Marti put the box from the bakery on the table.

"Oh, sister, so nice of you, bringing us a treat."

A pot of coffee was perking on a back burner. Doretta got out two chipped cups with a pink flower pattern and two green saucers. "Momma sure will be pleased to know you stopped by." She frowned with concentration as she poured some coffee and brought the cups to the table. Then she filled a small glass with milk, spilling some.

Marti tasted the coffee black. Some days Doretta's coffee was strong enough to stand a spoon in, others it tasted like coffee-flavored water. Today's was too good to dilute with milk or sugar.

Doretta sat across from her and pulled a piece of paper out of her apron pocket. The paper looked as if it had been folded and unfolded many times, and Doretta smoothed it out. "The Lord withholds no good things from those who walk in sincerity," she said, peering at a name she had written.

"Bring out the uncleanliness and return captives to the land." She reached for a pencil, moistened the lead with the tip of her tongue, and began printing in the large, uneven block lettering of a child. "You need to do somethin' about this one. 'Nother one of them Beelzebubs bringing the horsemen here."

Marti helped herself to a cheese danish and glanced at the paper that Doretta pushed toward her. Dr. Edwards, and the address of his temporary clinic. His recent move had brought his clinic within the boundaries of Doretta's concern.

"Pharaoh tell Gideon divide the spoils of dyed cloth so that Johal can drive in the tent peg and cover the Edomites with death rugs."

She waited. When Doretta mentioned horsemen and any name for the devil, she was talking about drugs and drug dealers. Marti knew the doctor was selling his free samples, but as far as she could determine, there were no other drugs in his clinic.

Doretta tapped a thick, blunt fingernail against the piece of paper. "Judas comes," she said. "And the dogs eat with the silver he plunders from Rachel's children."

Marti thought Doretta meant that the doctor was stealing.

Doretta tapped the paper again, then looked at her. "The leper is defiled by the one who is unclean. The horseman brings the children to captivity."

Horseman. Someone who sold dope. It could have something to do with prescriptions. Vik would know who could go about checking that out.

"Okay. I'll see what I can do about this."

"Soon. The horseman rides fast with destruction, brings the temple down at his feet."

"Soon," she promised. "Heard anything else about Danny Jones?"

Doretta looked so puzzled Marti was sure she must have forgotten everything they had talked about the last time she was here.

"Danny Jones?" Doretta hugged herself, hunching forward. "Danny Jones?" Then she gave Marti a smile. "Hit-and-run. Found him down in that ravine." She frowned. "One of them sneaky ones, quiet, listening and storing up what he hears. Got to watch out for them sneaky ones. Repay with destruction and be no longer a reproach. You are prey to their teeth."

Marti looked down at the piece of paper with the doctor's address. She had hoped for more. Judas and plunder. Something was making Edwards a wealthy man, and she wasn't convinced that it was legal. Then she thought of the young man in the morgue, shuddered as she remembered his mangled body. Quiet in life, according to Doretta, and now silent in death. Would she ever find out why he died?

23

As soon as roll call was over, Marti went upstairs. Court would be in session in about an hour and she and Vik seemed to be the only ones without a case on the docket. Slim and Cowboy had cleared out.

Vik was close to smiling as he read through a report. She disliked anything that looked as if it might be statistical data and couldn't understand Vik's penchant for orderly, itemized information, or his obvious enjoyment when he had to take random data and organize it into something that made sense.

She would never tell anyone, but she liked it when her mind could amble through scattered, seemingly unrelated facts and events and select those that she should pay attention to, until answers began falling into place. Intuition, Vik would say with scorn. Trust your instincts, Johnny would have said, impressed.

Vik was almost boisterous as he made a few phone calls and arranged to pick up some computerized prescription data.

"I think you missed your vocation, Jessenovik. You should have been an accountant, like Mrs. Edwards. Then you could tally used Band-Aids by blood type and add up all of the cotton swabs used by victims of gunshot wounds in Lake County in the past fifteen years."

Vik was so buoyed up by the prospect of searching through thousands of itemized drug purchases that his craggy face had a wild look. He wasn't paying any attention to what she was saying.

"You could even count the wrappers on all of the gauze pads used on puncture wounds that occurred in the northern quadrant of Lake County in the months of June, July, and August during World War II."

Vik still didn't respond. The look of excitement had been replaced with concern. "There was no clinic in that part of town for over three years," he said. "The women who live there need that place. It would be a damned shame if we found out Edwards was overprescribing controlled drugs."

"Is that why you're handling this yourself?"

"No need for anyone else to get involved unless there's something to it. What's your impression of Edwards?"

Marti thought of what Sharon had told her. "He seems to distance himself from people."

"Is that a polite way of saying you don't think he gives a damn about them?" Vik asked.

"He strikes me as someone who doesn't get personally involved," she said.

"Like someone who wouldn't get personally involved with a thirteen-year-old minor who was pregnant and brought here by a pimp?"

"I don't know. If you find something, it could make those computer diskettes a lot more important. I do not believe that nobody has a copy."

"They're out there," Vik said, with the conviction of an inveterate collector of data.

Marti was on the phone when Denise Stevens came in. Denise was as tall as Marti and about ten pounds heavier. She wore large hats to draw attention away from her body. Today's was a wide-brimmed, white straw with a big red rose.

"How are things going with Christina?" Marti asked.

"Slow. Very slow. I'm going to let her stay at the hospital the full thirty days and pray a lot. She's not a bad child, not even disrespectful, just hard. Damned shame to see a child that young so hardened by the streets. It takes time to break through that."

"Too bad we can't seem to intervene in early childhood,

when the abuse and neglect begins, and provide food, shelter, medical care, and adult supervision. We always seem to wait until they've been without that for so long they're in the juvenile system, and then, too often, it's too late."

Denise nodded in agreement. "You don't see as many of them as I do."

"One is more than enough." Odds were that Christina was already beyond anyone's ability to help her. The criminal world she had gotten herself into would rape her mind and her morals as well as her body. The legal system, with reformatories and group homes and foster care, was more likely to harm than to help her. It made Marti depressed just thinking about it.

"You might have put a dent in the kiddie-porn business," Denise said. "They confiscated enough film to stock a warehouse."

"Really? That's more than they told us."

"Mailing lists, too. They were even shipping stuff out of the country."

"Sounds like you owe me one, Stevens. Maybe you can help me with this dead kid, Danny Jones. He got locked up for about a month in Louisville. No priors as an adult. Think you can find out if there's a juvenile record? We've got no next of kin, no relatives, no nothing."

"Maybe we can put a composite in the newspaper," Denise suggested. "I can handle that for you. Takes a few days. By Thursday, maybe."

24

At 11:30 Marti and Vik met with Lieutenant Dirkowitz. After they brought him up to date on all four homicide investigations they headed over to the jail to see R.D. He had gotten out on bail but been arrested again a few hours later for having stolen plates on his car. Marti wasn't sure who had switched them, but she wouldn't put it past anyone working Vice.

R.D. still didn't want an attorney. Previous charges brought against him had been dropped before he got very far into the judicial process. This time there would be an arraignment. The judges here were conscientious and thorough. By the time one got finished explaining the charges, possible sentences, and R.D.'s rights under the law, Marti was certain he'd obtain legal representation.

"Two-bit punk," Vik grumbled as they took a shortcut through the county building. "Bringing runaway kids where I live and selling them into prostitution and pornography. Can't have that."

"Won't have it," she agreed.

"Good thing we had that fire, caught on to it before things went too far."

They didn't really know how far it had gone—if Christina and the unidentified victim were the only ones or if there had been others before them. Marti suspected the latter, but she knew what Vik meant. Vice had missed it because none of the prostitution or pornographic activity was happening here. Runaways and throwaways were everywhere these days. There were no missing persons reports on far too many of them because nobody wanted them back. God knew how many more little Jane Does were in cold storage. The precinct was always getting morgue shots on them.

"No," she said. "No way R.D.'s getting away with that here."

"Bastard," Vik muttered, his scowl deepening.

As soon as they walked into the interrogation room, Vik yanked a chair away from the table and sat down. Marti decided it might confuse R.D. if she remained calm this time. She leaned against the cream-colored wall, arms folded, willing herself to seem placid and benign.

Nobody spoke. She waited until R.D.'s foot began to jiggle, let the tempo increase before she said, "Things okay in here, R.D.?"

"Okay? What you mean okay? S'pose you done come up with somethin' else I'm s'posed to have done so's you can keep me here another twenty-four hours. Or just lock me up again soon as I make bail."

Marti spoke to Vik. "Man's let this baby-doll operation go to his head. Getting careless about where he gets his license plates. No telling what else he thinks he can get away with."

R.D. looked from one of them to the other. "What judge you gonna convince I'd put stolen plates on a twenty-five-thou-sand-dollar car?"

She considered that. "You know, R.D., you got something there. Gonna worry the hell out of him that you've got bold enough to think you can get away with something like that. This time you might even have outsmarted yourself."

"Them plates ain't mine. Car's registered just like it's s'posed to be."

"Brick take care of that for you this morning?" Marti said. She suppressed a smile as the tic near his eye picked up speed. "Heard they had to move you outta your cell when word got around that you preferred little girls."

The tic continued to twitch, and his Adam's apple began bobbing.

She enjoyed watching his controlled agitation. "Word's out on you now, man. Lot of your friends finding out there ain't nothing in your crotch to hold on to. No big boy's tool down there at all, just a little girl's toy."

With that they walked out of the room. The muscles in her neck and shoulders ached with tension. She was angry with R.D., with the juvenile system, with a lot of things. She walked the two blocks to the Y, ran nine half-mile laps, and took a shower. The sun felt hot enough to bake the top of her head as she returned to the precinct. She glanced at the headline in the *News-Times* as she walked past a machine that dispensed them.

SUSPECT IN CLINIC FIRE RELEASED.

She bought one. Old news again, inaccurate. It said R.D. was released Sunday, no mention of his re-arrest. Worse, it didn't mention the other charges against him—pandering, sexual assault, unlawful restraint, all felonies—and made it sound like he was getting away with murder. Maybe he was. An accomplice at least. Or, as she was beginning to think, the catalyst who got everything started in the first place. And by now, released again, back on the street.

The call came in at five minutes past two. R.D. had been shot in the pool hall that was his usual hangout. An ambulance was parked in front when Marti and Vik got there. Uniforms were keeping people away. Inside, music was blaring from a bystander's radio and a dozen people seemed to be talking at once.

A rookie uniform was trying to tell the crowd to quiet down. Furious because the rookie wasn't in complete control of the situation, Marti went over to him. She spoke just above a whisper. "You get this place quiet. Now. And everyone is to stay right where they are. And I had better have a clean scene of crime here."

The next time the rookie spoke he got everyone's attention and the radio was turned off.

R.D. was in the men's john. Marti hurried down a rear hallway, trying to ignore the warring odors of urine and disinfectant. The bathroom was small. R.D.'s feet stuck out of the one doorless stall. His face seemed even darker against the white porcelain urinal inches from his forehead. Ben Walker was kneeling beside him, blocking her view of the gunshot wound in R.D.'s midsection.

Ben spoke to the younger man hovering over him. "Send a strip."

R.D.'s vitals were relayed to the hospital.

"Diabetic," Ben said to his partner. "That's what you smelled on his breath. Smells like nail-polish remover."

He glanced up, saw Marti. "In shock. Getting him stable so we can transport. Gunshot. Small entrance wound, no exit. Not much bleeding. Small caliber. Abdomen."

Ben checked the IV drip, took R.D.'s pulse. "Still thready. Send another strip."

It took another five minutes to get an okay to move R.D. to the hospital. Marti watched as Ben worked on him. Ben had been a medic in 'Nam. She watched his hands, large and muscular, as he went about the tasks of getting R.D. stabilized. He was a very gentle man. Because she worked with so many men who always had to seem macho, that impressed her.

25

At five o'clock Tuesday morning Marti sat in the small waiting room near the intensive care unit at Lincoln Prairie General. Just before midnight, R.D. had undergone a second emergency operation for internal bleeding. About an hour ago he had come out of the anesthesia hallucinating and irrational. Instead of allowing Marti into his room to listen to his muttering and raving, his doctor had ordered a shot of morphine. Until R.D. was rational, nobody was allowed to see him except his mother, who was with him now. No one else had come to see him.

The room was too cool. Marti wished she had a sweater. The chairs were covered with vinyl and skimpily padded, with low backs, uncomfortable for sleeping. The back of her neck and her shoulders were beginning to ache. She massaged her neck, debating between going downstairs for another cup of vending machine coffee, weak with too much artificial creamer, or giving in to the tiredness and taking another nap.

She stood up, hunching and relaxing her shoulders, then took three giant steps between the rows of chairs lined against opposite walls. She reached the table with the lamp and magazines with two more steps, then took six long strides in the opposite direction to the hall door. This must be what it's like to be locked in a cell, she thought.

They had no suspects in the shooting, no idea of a particular reason why someone would have wanted to shoot R.D. yesterday afternoon, and no weapon. She sat, legs sprawled, and closed her eyes.

A first-shift janitor jolted her with the squeak of a wheel as his bucket rolled along. The squeaking stopped and he clamped a ringer over the mop. After a few minutes the bucket rolled farther away. She was just closing her eyes again and trying to ease her neck into a semicomfortable position when Vik came in. The pouches under his eyes were larger and darker than usual. He'd been up most of the night too, questioning suspects and going over the preliminary reports.

"Hi, kid. How's it going? Talk to R.D. yet? What are our chances of getting a deathbed statement?"

"Slim to none. But it doesn't look like he's going to die. You find out anything yet?"

"Are you kidding? Know how many prints you can lift in a men's john?"

Since she was sure he knew, she decided to guess. "Seventeen full sets, six partials?"

"Not even close." He sat down in the chair next to her. "Damp in that bathroom, and a lot of traffic. Fifteen partials, three full sets right hand, five full sets left hand, six thumbs, and twelve miscellaneous fingers."

He didn't sound tired, even if he looked it.

"If you keep sounding so wide-awake and cheerful, Jessenovik, I'm going to go eat three stale cream-filled donuts from the junk-food machine and throw up in your lap."

"Here." He held out a Thermos. "Stopped by the house on the way over. My wife made it."

"Real coffee? You're forgiven." She held the cup with both hands, inhaling the aroma as it cooled.

"I've questioned everyone but Linda and Brick," Vik said. "Seems like they've run to ground."

"Makes sense if this is some kind of warning or retaliation. No telling what R.D.'s into in Chicago. Be nice to know where they're holed up."

"Their bail's been revoked and we've got warrants out on them."

"No leads on who might have shot him?"

"Nothing." Vik stood up, paced to the wall, and came back. He stared at the chair. "They don't want you to stay here long, do they?" he said, sitting down. "I can't decide whether R.D. was shot by some amateur with a grudge or if it's connected to any of our other homicides."

"Think it could have been one of his girls?"

Taking out a collapsible cup, Vik poured himself some of the coffee and gave Marti a refill. "Nah. Glodine's still not in any condition to have climbed out of that bathroom window. It's high up, faces an alley. It had to be someone agile and strong enough to grab on to the ledge, get some kind of grip from the wall, and hoist himself up and over to exit the building. It wasn't easy. I did pay Glodine a little visit last night. She didn't look or act as if she'd gotten any extra exercise yesterday. No alibi, but I don't think she's the one."

"Well, I don't think Linda shot him either. He's still the best meal ticket she's got."

"And Brick is an unknown. He's been with R.D. for twelve, fifteen years," Vik said. "We've picked him up a couple dozen times but never been able to charge him with anything and make it stick. Too bad it wasn't one of the women," he complained. "Someone waits for him in a john that hasn't been cleaned since the plumbing was installed, shoots him in the gut with a .22-caliber weapon that didn't do too much damage at close range. Aiming for the head or heart would have made some sense, but shooting through fifty pounds of fat and expecting to hit something vital doesn't, unless the perp either knew nothing about guns or wasn't trying to kill him."

"Someone who was angry, maybe." With the angry ones you had to get to the motive. "There could be any number of people out there with reasons for wanting R.D. shot." She thought of yesterday's newspaper headline saying he'd been released. That was about the only thing he'd had time to do lately—get arrested twice and get out of jail. "But if they were angry, you'd think they'd want to make sure he was dead. He sure didn't get shot because he ticked off one of his associates in Chicago. This isn't how any of the big boys take care of business."

Marti sipped the coffee. "Leave it to R.D. The man can't even get shot right."

"We found some papers at his house last night that weren't there before," Vik said. "Someone had to have brought them in since Saturday. I can't even guess why anyone would do that so soon after we took the place apart."

"Odd," Marti agreed. "But we're talking about someone dumb enough not to get an attorney. Did you find anything?"

"Enough to make you think. His income damn near tripled in the last year or so, and he didn't know what to do with that kind of money. Smart, though. He must have hit every jeweler and every men's store at every mall in Chicago. He bought stereo equipment like you wouldn't believe, two televisions with fifty-two-inch screens. Went to the bank, too."

Vik yawned. "Chicago cops hit his place there. Found enough cocaine for recreational use but not enough to deal. A little heroin, too, probably for Glodine and Linda. That's usually what they get their girls hooked on. Slim and Cowboy are looking at the unlabeled porn films now. They're having stills made of the little girls, but they haven't seen our Jane Doe or Christina yet." He shook the Thermos, let her have the last of the coffee. "We'll circulate the photographs, see if anything turns up."

"God, I hope not," Marti said. "We still got someone coming in today to look at the clinic-fire victim?"

"Far as I know," Vik said.

She leaned back and exhaled slowly. "Damn." It was hard enough dealing with the families of the deceased when she'd had a decent night's sleep. It would be worth it if they got a positive ID, though.

* * *

At 7:30 Vik went downstairs to get a Chicago newspaper. While he was gone, R.D.'s mother came to the waiting room. Although Marti had never seen Mrs. Davies before she arrived here last night, her face seemed familiar. It only took a few minutes for Marti to place her as a real estate agent whose picture occasionally appeared in the classified ads.

This morning, after a night in her son's room, Mrs. Davies looked as if she had been interrupted during a business conference. She was carrying a maroon leather briefcase and wearing a navy blue suit with a white tailored silk blouse. Her brown hair was cut short and combed in feathery layers. She was a tall woman with an attitude that suggested she was used to being in charge.

"Officer MacAlister. You're still here."

It seemed unlikely that R.D.'s mother would contribute much information. "Yes, ma'am. How is he?"

"Regaining consciousness. You're waiting to question him?"

"Yes."

"This is the first time I've seen him in a month. I've been on a cruise in the Caribbean. He stops by during the week to see what's cooking and cut the grass, or check the fluid levels in my car."

Marti didn't feel much like thinking of R.D. as a human being, and didn't want to hear about his domestic attributes.

"I'm aware of some of his . . ." Mrs. Davies hesitated. "Activities. His father was a gambler, did time for armed robbery. Easy to get rid of a shiftless husband. A lot harder when it's your own flesh and blood."

"Did he ever bring anyone along when he stopped by to visit you?"

"No. He always came alone."

"A lot of parents wouldn't have had anything to do with him."

"I couldn't do that. Didn't have but the one. He's all I've got."

A nurse came to the door. "Detective, Doctor says you can see Mr. Davies for five minutes."

Marti followed the nurse to a room with a wide window along the inner wall so that anyone at the nurses' station could look in. There was a tube in R.D.'s nose and an IV in his arm. He was catheterized. One hand was free. He gave Marti the middle finger.

She smiled. "Nice to see you, too. Know who did this?"

"Don't you?" He spoke just louder than a whisper. "Smart-assed cop like you s'posed to know everything."

R.D. still had an attitude problem. She decided it was time they reached an understanding. "If you don't tell me what you know, R.D., I'm going to have you manacled to your bed and have a guard posted who will be down the hall taking a leak when whoever did this comes back to finish the job."

"Tough Chicago cop." He was trying to sound flippant, but couldn't quite hide the uncertainty in his eyes.

"That what you want?"

He swallowed and looked up at the IV dripping fluids and medication into his vein. "Never saw him."

"This got anything to do with the baby dolls you been bringing here?"

"Don't think so."

She noted the admission.

"Somebody got it in for you?"

"Don't know."

She began noticing the odor in the room—an antiseptic smell, like medicine or iodine and alcohol, but sour, too. "Give me a description."

"Can't. Came up from behind. Think he was short. Don't know. Didn't pay attention. Happened too fast. Thought he bumped into me." He tried to suppress a cough, and she watched the pain seep into his eyes. Then he swallowed, his face contorting as he tugged at the tube going down his throat. He closed his eyes.

"You sure it was a man?"

"Don't know. Don't feel so good. Get the hell out of here, Mac."

She watched as the pain kept surfacing, until the nurse said she had to leave.

26

After the coolness of the hospital, the early morning heat hit Marti like a blast from a furnace when she went outside. Sprinklers were squirting water on the narrow strips of grass that flanked the hospital wings, and sparrows chirped in the hedge near the main exit. The breeze blowing across her face promised another ninety-degree day.

When she got to the precinct, Cowboy was engaged in a seek-and-destroy mission.

"Damned earwigs," he complained, spraying insecticide along the baseboards. "Time for our late July, early August reinfestation."

His muscles strained against his shirt as he crouched near the wall. Cowboy couldn't stand bugs, and Marti suspected he was at least half afraid of spiders. She had no intention of figuring out how to catch one and find out for sure.

She typed up a report and got ready to go home for a few hours' sleep. Before she could leave, Slim escorted an elderly woman to her desk.

"This is Mrs. Robertson, Marti, Janey Willis's great-aunt. She came in by bus from Memphis this morning."

So, their Jane Doe had been positively identified.

"Janet Petrosky was with her when she identified Janey."

Sometimes Slim did show more sensitivity than she gave him credit for. Petrosky considered comforting the bereaved part of her job, and would have made the ordeal as easy as possible.

Marti focused on the aunt, trying not to feel too tired to talk with her. She was a tiny woman. Her dark face was scored with deep wrinkles, her eyes red-rimmed, probably as much from fatigue as from crying. There was a weary sort of acceptance in the way she sat, back straight but shoulders bowed. Her hands were old, bony, with protruding veins and large knuckles that suggested years of manual work.

She wore a shiny black dress with a starched crocheted collar and cuffs that could be removed for laundering. Marti could remember her mother wearing collars and cuffs like that years ago, on the dresses she saved for church.

"I'm very sorry about Janey, Mrs. Robertson." The woman shouldn't have had to travel so far by bus. They would have to see to it that she had a sleeper on Amtrak going back, or a plane ticket if she wanted to fly. "When's the last time you saw her?"

"Middle of June. Not long after school was out. She was getting held back again. Real upset about that. Always kinda slow in school. Couldn't keep up like her sisters did. Teacher say she need special help, that maybe next year they be able to get some for her." Tears brimmed in her eyes. She wiped at them with the corner of a rumpled handkerchief. "We thought she was with her sister Maddie, in Chattanooga."

"Why did you think that?"

"Said that was where she was going when she left."

"Did she usually go to Chattanooga on her own, or did her sister come for her?"

"Janey go by herself. Stayed there all last summer, too. Got herself a job baby-sitting. Bought herself some clothes for school and bring her momma home a little money besides. Good girl, Janey. Her daddy die five, six years ago 'cause his sugar get too high, left Kessie, her momma, with seven to look after. Kessie clean at the nursing home most days and work nights too when she can. Her pressure's up now with all of this. I come 'cause ain't no way she can take off from work."

"How do you think Janey got here?"

"Think she got some notion or other in her head to come this way because her best friend visited relatives in Chicago last year. She say she don't ever want to go back to school no more. Younger ones tease her about getting left back, even though Kessie tell 'em not too. Mighta thought she could find work here. Janey like her momma. Ain't nothin' lazy nor shiftless about her."

The results of the autopsy had not been released outside of the department. Mrs. Robertson had not been told yet that Janey was pregnant. It was important that it not reach the newspapers until they determined whether it had anything to do with why Janey had been in Dr. Edwards's clinic. If Janey left home in mid-June, she'd gotten pregnant before she came here.

"Did Janey like boys?"

The old woman smiled. "She real taken with the school principal's son. Everyone tease her about that. 'How someone like that gonna come courtin' the likes of you,' they say. Janey just smile, like she believe it would happen."

Marti reached into her pocket and took out a plastic bag containing the ring that she had found at R.D.'s house.

The old woman took the ring in her hand and rubbed the thin metal band with her fingertip. "She be havin' this. For true."

"That was Janey's?"

The woman nodded. Tears spilled on her dress, soaking in. Then she sniffed, wiped her eyes. "Junk it be," she said. "But Janey, she be my favorite. Always comin' over doin' some little thing for me. Help me cook, wash my floor, or pull weeds in my garden. Never ask me for nothin', not once." She fingered the ring, held it tight. "Do I got to be givin' it back?"

"For a while, but I'll see that you get it."

"Was this little carnival at school. Kids throw things in cans, get little prizes. Janey, she say, 'Aunt Nedra, you can get that beanbag through that hole, sure you can.' And my arthritis so bad I can hardly raise my arm some days. But she say I can, so I throws it, and this be the prize. I give it to her and she wears it on a little chain 'round her neck. Sweet little girl, Janey." She clutched the ring again. "Just as sweet as she could be. No need of this happenin' to her. No need at all."

"You look tired, Mrs. Robertson. Have you got a motel reservation?"

"Bus comes back this way this evening. I'll be going back then. I got the insurance policy. Be enough to bury her here, not enough to take her back home with me."

Slim came over. "Mrs. Robertson, I didn't know you planned to go back so soon. And I didn't think you should be alone at a time like this. I sort of took it upon myself to arrange for you to stay with my mother for a few days." Marti glanced at him. "My daddy was a minister, ma'am. Now that he's gone, Momma lives alone and she's looking forward to having some company. She'll be real mad with me if you don't come, think I must've forgot my manners and got to actin' like some uppity police officer again. Always after me, ma'am, for not spending enough time with her, ever since my sister got married and moved to California. Hard to get over there sometimes with this work an' all. You will stay with her? She's got a pot of greens on already and I had to drop off some chickens on my way to work. And she promised to have a pineapple upside-down cake for me when I brought you home."

Slim was at his most charming, reeking of Obsession and looking like a little boy who had played hooky from Sunday school and had to do a good deed to atone. With a little more encouragement and the mention of a traveling Baptist preacher, the elderly woman accepted. By noon there was a coffee can on the sergeant's desk with a sign asking for contributions to get Janey and her aunt back home.

27

Marti took Mrs. Robertson to a nearby restaurant for a hot lunch while Slim called his mother and made arrangements for the woman to stay there. Marti had known Slim was lying when he made the offer, but was glad that he did. Another overnight bus ride without any rest in between would have been exhausting, and Slim had handled the situation without embarrassing anyone. Marti was back at her desk considering the possibility of sleep when the phone rang.

"Officer MacAlister, it's me, Carmen."

Because she was tired, it took a second to remember that Carmen was Dr. Edwards's receptionist, and to connect the voice with the young woman she had spoken with in Chicago. "Are you in Lincoln Prairie?"

"No. I'm going to stay here with my grandmother. The lady you told me to see will help me get enrolled in a medical-assistant training program."

"Glad to hear it." She recalled her initial impression that Carmen was fast, loose, and selfish. Instead, that seemed to better describe Teresa Martinez. "Keep in touch. Let me know how things are going."

"There is something else I should tell you." She sounded uncertain.

Marti waited.

"It's about Teresa. My grandmother says you should know."

Marti stifled a yawn.

"Teresa got pregnant just before she graduated from high

school. It was not her fiancé's child, and even if it was, she did not want to get married," Carmen said, still sounding reluctant to speak. "Someone told her that if her period was late, Dr. Edwards might do a D and C in his office. But only if she convinced him that a baby would really mess up her life, and if she had the five hundred dollars. Afterwards, he gave her birth control pills. At first she was grateful that he did this. Then she decided that he had been wrong to help her, that maybe her mother and brother should know what had happened. Her family is very religious. Then she wanted to work for the doctor. When he gave her a job she wanted to get paid whether she went in or not and asked me to work when she didn't feel like it."

Marti resisted an impulse to put her head on her desk. Some doctors did D and Cs in their offices. Sharon had had one done that way in February, but not to terminate a pregnancy.

"What happens at the clinic on those Thursdays when Teresa would work?"

"Sometimes it is because Dr. Edwards does a D and C. Sometimes it is because he does not want me to know who the patient is—or that is what Teresa told me, that she was the only one he trusted."

But Teresa wasn't supposed to be there on the Thursday she died.

"You were scheduled to work the night of the fire?"

"Yes, but the doctor said no. I called Teresa to ask why not, but she had already left home."

"What time were you notified?"

"Dr. Edwards called about quarter to six."

"And there were regular patients scheduled that night?"

"Yes. Four. The first one at 7:15."

Marti switched the receiver to her other ear. Apparently, Edwards had decided he needed Teresa at 5:45. He left the clinic around six. When he returned at 6:50 the clinic was burning. Why had he called Teresa? Marti didn't want to believe that Edwards knew Janey would be there. Had R.D. brought the victim to the clinic so that Edwards could perform a D and C? And if so, why had Janey arrived when she did, and not after Edwards had seen his other patients?

"Is there anything else I should know?" Marti asked.

"I am not sure."

"Tell me anyway."

Marti waited.

"A few weeks before she died, Teresa told Dr. Edwards that he must pay us twenty dollars an hour. He said that he would, but a few days later he was angry, said that now, thanks to her, someone else was trying to take what was his."

"Did she know what he meant?"

"No. She did not understand. He had just lost his keys. Teresa said maybe he thought she had taken them, but there was no reason why she should."

"I thought Teresa was the one who lost the keys," Marti said.

"No, it was Dr. Edwards."

Marti rubbed her eyes. She didn't have enough new information to question Edwards yet, but she would have to talk with him again.

She repeated the conversation to Vik.

"Need to talk with him," Vik agreed. "Be a damned shame if he's involved with R.D. Let me put in another call to Fraud. See what they've found on those prescription records. They looked suspicious to me."

Vik called Fraud, then notified the lieutenant. By three o'clock they knew that Edwards was overprescribing controlled drugs and Vik had a list of patients, medications, dates, and quantities to confirm it.

While they were waiting, Marti put in a call to the state licensing agency. She didn't find out anything about Edwards, but the clinic where he had practiced before coming to Lincoln Prairie was closed. There had been evidence of prescription-drug abuse and insurance fraud.

"I want Edwards brought in," the lieutenant said when Marti gave him the news. "Get a warrant on the drug offenses, but I want you to pursue possible charges for contributing to the abuse of Janey Willis. I want this stopped, now."

28

When Marti and Vik arrived at the clinic, six patients were sitting in the molded plastic chairs.

"Official business," Vik announced, displaying his shield.

Mrs. Johnson glared at him. "Doctor is seeing patients."

"Yes, ma'am, I know. Sorry, but we have to interrupt him."

"I understand," she said, giving the women who were waiting an apologetic shrug.

"Perhaps you could reschedule them, ma'am," Vik suggested. "This could take a while."

Mrs. Johnson turned to Marti. "There's someone in with him. You'll have to wait about five minutes."

Mrs. Johnson didn't say anything when Vik went outside to make sure the doctor couldn't leave by any other exit. When evidence techs arrived and asked to see the storeroom, she said, "Dear Lord, it's come to this." She looked as if she were about to cry as she showed them down the hall.

Marti went in to speak with Edwards as soon as his patient left the office. Edwards came out of the examining room wearing a white lab coat. When Vik ambled in, Edwards looked up to stare at him. The doctor's thin lips were compressed, his expression haughty. There was no warmth in his face. While Marti couldn't think of him as a compassionate man, she wondered how his patients felt about him, whether they would come forward to defend his character once he was charged. Mrs. Johnson seemed to think well of him. Carmen didn't dislike him. How did the others feel?

Vik took a step forward. "You're under arrest." He took a card out of his pocket and read the doctor his rights.

Edwards didn't seem surprised. "How long will this take?"

"Hard to say," Vik replied. "These things take time."

Edwards accompanied them to the precinct without protest. They charged him with the prescription-drug offenses and with selling samples, and, with the unofficial help of the state's attorney's office, had the Illinois Department of Professional Registration delay questioning him until tomorrow. That justified holding him in jail overnight without bail.

It was 7:15 when Dr. Edwards's lawyer arrived. Marti and Vik joined them at the round table.

The attorney half rose, extending his hand. "David Weinstein. Sorry for the delay. I had to drive up from Chicago."

He was a handsome, middle-aged man with a receding hairline.

"Well, now. I'm sure we can resolve this without too much difficulty. What do we have?"

Vik opened a manila folder. "So far, we have forty-nine little problems here, Mr. Weinstein." He began to read from the list that Fraud had provided. "Adamson, Jane, main drug of choice Benzedrine. Clayton, Arintha, Valium. Diaz, Rosa, Preludin . . ."

The doctor was wiping his forehead with his shirt sleeve when Weinstein interrupted. "Okay, okay. That's adequate. Needless to say, my client will not respond."

Smiling, Marti and Vik stood up. "We'll leave you two to consult," Vik said. "Sorry we have to hold him, but the Department of Professional Registration can't have anyone here to talk with him until sometime tomorrow."

Lieutenant Dirkowitz was eating a salad when they arrived at his office.

"So, they know what we've got with the prescriptions?"

"Right," Vik said.

"Good. State will have to suspend his license for that, too

flagrant. And since we found that out so fast, and he knows now that we have been investigating him—"

"He's got a whole night in a jail cell to wonder what else we might know," Vik added.

"What do you want?" Marti asked.

The lieutenant offered them each a can of diet pop while he considered. "Realistically, we might not get anywhere determining what Edwards's connection is with R.D. and the minor, but I want you to pursue that anyway. The state's attorney's office pursues these sex crime cases aggressively. If we can give them enough, I think they'll prosecute Edwards too. They will definitely nail R.D. this time. Good work on that."

Marti sipped at the pop without enjoying the taste while the lieutenant finished off his salad.

"Now," Dirkowitz said, reaching for the grenade on his desk. "You're not making much progress with the four homicides. We need a break here, something. What have you got?"

"We want to lean on Reverend Halloran," Vik said. "He's the best suspect we have in the arson."

"Go for it."

"We're at square one with Jones and Price," Marti admitted. "We'll be hitting the streets again, first thing tomorrow."

"Good enough." Dirkowitz didn't sound pleased. "I'm most concerned with nailing the arsonist, but I expect results on the other two also."

He dropped the grenade on the desk with a loud bang.

29

When Marti returned to her desk, she glanced at the reminder she had taped to her answering machine. *Tuesday. Joanna. Softball. 6 P.M.* It was 9:15. She had missed another game. Opening her file drawer, she took out all of the folders relevant to the four homicides and began reading through them.

Vik tapped his pencil on a sheet of paper half filled with his illegible handwriting. When the lead broke he threw the pencil across the room, aiming it like a dart.

"I feel like we're going in circles," he said. "Everybody's like your buddy Isaac. None of them have seen nothing. None of them know nothing. Nobody recognizes Jones. Nobody knows Janey Willis. Nobody knows what in the hell Teresa Martinez was doing in that clinic at 6:45." He aimed another pencil. "Nothing!"

Marti read through her notes on Carmen's call. "The keys," she said. "Carmen says Edwards lost his keys. He says Teresa lost hers. I believe Carmen."

"So?"

"It's a lie. I've got something that I'm sure he's lying about."

"Great. Now tell me why it's important."

Marti didn't know, and she wasn't even sure how to find out. She kept going over the reports. "We also know that something happened, probably about five-thirty that afternoon, to change Edwards's plans for the evening. Question is, does it have anything to do with why Janey was there. Or with why Teresa came in early."

Vik snapped a pencil in half. "And you're sure the doctor will tell us, right? Those two girls sure can't."

"Janey was pregnant. Cyprian says the pregnancy was normal. Why was she there? Did someone call at 5:30 and make an appointment? People know he does D and Cs. Or was this a routine arrangement with R.D.? Did he take care of R.D.'s girls?"

"No evidence," Vik said.

"There was also a break-in of some kind. When I was at Edwards's house I saw the marks from a forced entry on one of the cabinets his wife keeps her antique knickknacks in. I checked. It wasn't reported."

Scowling, Vik pushed back his chair. He went to Cowboy's desk, took all of the pencils from his pencil holder, and fed them into the electric sharpener. The whining grind set Marti's teeth on edge.

"I agree," she said. "The more we find out the less we seem to know."

There was a sharp rap on glass and she looked up to see a uniform standing at the open door to the squad room. "A Mrs. Johnson to see you, ma'am."

Dr. Edwards's receptionist came in, still wearing the pink-and-blue-striped smock she wore at the clinic. She had been crying. Looked like a citizen's complaint.

Vik eyed the open door and took a step toward it as if he was going to leave. Marti got up, ready to physically restrain him. No way was she dealing with a crying woman alone this time. Then she noticed the dark, portly man still standing in the hall.

"Mr. Johnson?" she asked, hopeful.

"No," he intoned, stepping into the room and pausing as if he expected applause. "I am the Reverend Rutherford B. Hurley."

She didn't recognize him or his name. "Baptist?"

"Gideon Baptist Church, Kenosha." Marti thought he was too short to have such a deep voice. Every time he spoke she almost looked around to see where the giant ventriloquist was.

The voice must come right from the belly—sideways, he would not have been able to get through the doorway.

"Well, Reverend, I hope that little search I ordered this afternoon doesn't mean I'm out of fellowship." She hadn't meant to say that out loud. "That means excommunicated," she whispered to Vik.

The reverend was not amused. "Mrs. Johnson asked me to accompany her on a most difficult task. She came to me this evening in dire need of spiritual guidance and moral direction. I advised her to come to you because it is the correct, if difficult, thing to do."

Marti was tired enough to get silly. Maybe if she just listened and didn't say much . . . "Would you like to sit down?"

Vik yanked out his chair and plopped down with a loud sigh. The reverend glared at him, then spoke to Marti. "We must commit ourselves to the dissemination of the truth."

Vik covered his mouth and made a strangled, snorting noise, trying not to laugh. Marti raised her cup at him in a careful but threatening gesture.

Mrs. Johnson took the chair beside Marti's desk and leaned toward her, clutching her purse so tightly the fabric was about to tear. "Doctor Edwards is such a good man, Officer. Such a kind, decent person."

Marti nodded. Maybe Mrs. Johnson wasn't going to complain about the mess the search team made at the clinic.

"He wouldn't do anything wrong. It's that wife of his." Mrs. Johnson's chin jutted out. "He is not a bad person, Officer MacAlister."

Marti nodded again. She had no idea why Mrs. Johnson would need her minister with her to say this. She knew if she opened her mouth she would giggle. Vik got up and turned to the window. His shoulders began to shake. They were both ready to explode with laughter, and not one thing was funny. They were tired.

The Reverend Mr. Hurley cleared his throat. He looked as

if he were about to address the nation. "I have advised Mrs. Johnson to come forward at this time because she is a law-abiding citizen and a faithful member of my congregation. As Christians we must choose the morally correct thing to do, give example to the unbeliever, and bring the godless to justice." That said, he folded his hands over his belly.

Mrs. Johnson opened her purse. "I copied these. She doesn't think I know how. Always did that herself. Doesn't think I'm smart like she is. The inventory file is mine. The others are hers."

"Four diskettes," Marti said, staring at them.

"I copied hers because I thought the doctor might need them one day."

The way Mrs. Johnson was clutching them, she might be changing her mind about handing them over.

"Mrs. Johnson, may I have them? Please."

"I knew it would come to this. I knew she would bring that man trouble soon as she told me to sell those free samples. I knew that greedy, selfish woman would drag that good man down." She tapped the disks. "Dirty Wrights. That's all any of them ever were. Ain't enough she can buy that can change that. She's the one. These will prove it."

"Yes, Mrs. Johnson. I'm sure it will. Now please, if you'll just let me have them."

"I just know these will tell you everything that woman did," Mrs. Johnson said, handing them over.

30

When Marti walked into the kitchen Wednesday morning, Sharon was waiting for her.

"Girl, where were you last night? I waited up until Arsenio was over. You were gone when I got up yesterday morning, didn't come home for supper. The kids haven't seen you in a couple of days."

Sharon's caftan swirled as she went to the counter to make coffee. "I'm sure glad I beat you to the coffeepot."

Marti had been hungry before Sharon came in. Now she felt like throwing her English muffins into the wastebasket. She hadn't seen Joanna or Theo in two days, except to go into their rooms while they were sleeping. She hadn't had time for them. Again.

"Everything okay?" she asked.

Sharon put the mugs, Equal, and skimmed milk on the table. "Joanna came home from her softball game Saturday night with a headache. Stayed at the party for about thirty minutes and went upstairs. Chris was there, too—that running back I was telling you about. Half a head shorter than she is, but he'll catch up. And any idiot could see that she likes him."

"I'll talk to her," Marti said. But when? "I'm supposed to go to Theo's Cub Scout meeting tonight and talk about my job." Ben was going to fill in for her if she couldn't make it. "I'll come home afterwards, promise."

"Oh, Marti." Sharon gave her a hug. "Girl, the kids are all right. You don't spend this much time away from them that often. I worry more that you're missing out on something than

I worry about them. You haven't made it to any of Joanna's games lately and she's really pitching good. Hitting, too."

"Case has to break soon," she said. "I miss those softball games a lot."

"Season's not over for another two or three weeks. And guess what? I've got some good news. Went to court yesterday."

Marti had forgotten about that.

"Girl, the judge told Franklin that he wasn't giving me enough money. Gave back some of that money he took away the last time because Franklin's got a raise since then. Franklin was in shock, do you hear me? First time that man hasn't gotten his way since he came out of the womb."

Sharon did a little dance. The colors in her caftan looked even brighter when she stepped into the sunlight. Marti hugged her. "I'm so glad something finally went right for you."

"Now you just make it home for a couple of hours tonight, Miss Marti. We got a little celebrating to do. Guess you were right about that lawyer."

"Promise," she said again. "I'll try."

The house was still cool, but Marti felt sticky and uncomfortable by the time she backed the car down the driveway. She had logged in five hours' sleep last night after spending Monday night at the hospital waiting to talk to R.D., and she still felt tired. She hadn't spent any time with her kids in two weeks. And now she was going back to the hospital to see Christina. There were a lot of questions that needed answers, but so far, Christina wasn't telling anyone anything. Marti didn't think this would be her lucky day, but she had to try.

She avoided the central desk, took a service elevator to the third floor, and went to the juvenile dependency ward. She identified herself through the intercom and the lock buzzed. The corridor leading to the nurses' station and wards was deserted. She took a deep breath, bracing herself for another encounter with a hostile, street-wise little girl.

A nurse wearing a yellow smock came toward her. "Detective MacAlister, am I glad to see you. I was just going to call Denise Stevens. Maybe you could have a talk with Christina. I think she's stolen a stuffed animal from one of the other girls. She won't give it back."

"Are you sure she stole it?"

"It's Christina's word against Ashleigh's, but Christina has already taken several things that didn't belong to her."

"How is she? Other than guilty."

"Still completely withdrawn," the nurse said. She pushed a button and a buzzer sounded again. "She'll never get off this ward if she keeps stealing. I hate to have to make a fuss about this stuffed toy. She seems so attached to it. But she does have to give it back if it's not hers. She hasn't had any visitors."

The curtains were pulled shut in Christina's room. The nurse opened them. "Nice day, Christina," she said as she left the room. "Take a look outside."

Christina was in bed, hugging a stuffed brown bear with a tan plaid sweater and a matching cap pinned at a jaunty angle to its head. Its eyes were big and seemed wise and sad.

"What's his name?"

Christina didn't answer right away. Then, with a convulsive squeeze, she whispered, "MacTavish."

"Suits him," Marti said.

Such a little girl. She couldn't be five feet tall, and so thin. Reaching out, Marti smoothed Christina's hair. "Good" hair, straight, not kinky. R.D., or Preppy, had wanted a specific type. Black, but seeming almost white.

Christina's family had been notified. They had not reported her missing. According to Denise, the mother had said, "Keep her there. Trouble, that chile, nothin' but trouble, almost since she was borned. Come back and she'll jus' be trouble again."

Marti gave the bear a little squeeze. Soft, and huggable. Exactly what Christina needed. "I hear some kid says he's hers."

"Lying bitch," Christina muttered. She clutched the bear tighter.

"Tell me how you got him."

"Came last night," Christina whispered. "Nurse brought it in. Don't know where it came from. Ain't giving it away, neither. Lying little bitch got a room full of shit she don't need. Gonna whip her ass she don't leave what's mine alone."

"I'll see what I can do. Be right back."

She found the nurse in the yellow smock, waited while she contacted the nurses on the night shift, and talked with the one who had given Christina the bear.

"Someone left it at the front desk for Christina. I'm glad it really is hers."

Marti went back to Christina's room, told her everything was straightened out. "But if you expect people to believe you when something is yours, you're going to have to stop stealing. You need anything?"

"Tampax," Christina whispered.

Marti got some sanitary napkins from the nurse and made a trip to the drugstore for the tampons. She brought back some candy bars, too.

31

When Marti got back to the precinct, Vik had a dozen photographs on his desk lined up in rows of four. He was just sitting there, looking at them. Marti got a cup of coffee, then stood behind him. Young girls, none of them familiar, but the similarities were there. Delicate features, "good" hair. Skin almost light enough to pass for white.

"What have we got?"

"Stills from the porn films confiscated at R.D.'s apartment in Chicago. Two have been identified." He pointed them out. "We don't know who the other ten are or where they might be now. Look at the expressions on their faces. Scared, all of them, but smiling. Enough to make you sick."

She went to her desk, put her head in her hands, and said every curse she knew. "We got anything on the film?"

"Homemade. Period." Vik sounded as dejected as she felt. "And R.D. could have got it anywhere."

"We can't tie any of these girls to him, Vik? Just Christina?"

"Slim and Cowboy are talking with Vice in Chicago. They might come up with something."

She swore again. "Nothing's coming together. Did Fraud find anything on those diskettes?"

"They didn't waste any time. Got someone in here last night. Insurance fraud. But that doesn't help us with the arson or tell us one damned thing that we need to know about the dead girls."

"Vik, I think we've got to assume Edwards was involved

with R.D., and not just because anyone who commits fraud would contribute to the abuse of a minor child."

"The preponderance of evidence," Vik agreed reluctantly.

"It's the only possible reason for her being there, Vik, Hippocratic oath be damned. There just isn't any other explanation. Not that it explains why she died, or who killed her."

"R.D. was bringing little girls here!" Vik exploded. "He was sheltering and pandering them."

"And Edwards must have been providing medical care."

Vik swore.

"I know." A whole chain of child abuse, and Dr. Edwards had contributed instead of intervening. And they still lacked the hard evidence to bring charges.

"Damn." She tasted the coffee. It was awful. "I wish you'd stay away from the coffeepot, Jessenovik. Diesel fuel tastes better than this."

"If a certain female officer would get her butt in here early enough to—"

"Don't even say it," she warned.

Vik settled into a sulking silence.

She gave the coffee to the spider plant and reached for a stack of folders, flipping through the contents without bothering to read anything. "I suppose the doctor and his wife have been released?"

"Sometime today."

"Bet they skip town."

"Maybe," Vik said.

"We can't nail them for anything relating to the juveniles." She slouched down, stretching her legs. "Insurance claims, adult junkies, that's what's important, not some twelve-year-old making porn movies and hustling for some nickel-and-dime pimp."

"Right," Vik agreed. "So don't bust an artery bleeding over it. Doesn't look like there's any way we can get him for that. I've been talking to some of the members of Reverend Halloran's group, trying to break his alibi. That bunch is rabid where

Edwards is concerned. If there were any way of implicating him, one of them would have come up with it by now."

"You get anywhere with the reverend's alibi?"

"No, it's his word, and his wife's. But I found out the daughter wasn't where she said she was. Maybe I have got some good news. You heard the latest on R.D.?"

"Don't know if I want to."

"He might be paralyzed. Permanently."

"R.D.? Why?"

"Got some kind of infection in his spine," Vik explained. "You know how diabetics are. Don't heal so good."

"Be damned. I hope he's in one hell of a lot of pain."

"Going to question him again?" Vik asked.

"Probably not. We need evidence. Got enough to charge him with having Christina at his house. Should get some mileage out of that. Pandering is a felony. There's also unlawful restraint, one to three, and criminal sexual assault, mandatory three to seven. If Christina would just talk." This wasn't enough. There had to be something she hadn't uncovered, something she had overlooked.

"Crippled, huh? Can't you see him tooling around States-ville Prison in a wheelchair, Vik? I wonder if they have access ramps for the handicapped. Cons would make a little girl out of him real quick."

She went back to her files on Ruth Price and Danny Jones. "Nobody's claimed the Jones body yet?"

"Nope. His composite will hit the newspapers tomorrow. Maybe someone who knows him will see it."

Probably not, she thought. She didn't feel optimistic about anything. "Maybe if we could get him a little closer to R.D. . . . ."

"We know he hung around the pool hall," Vik said. "Don't know if there's much sense in going back there again, though. Those people forget their own names when you say 'cop.' "

"And everyone in there was clean when R.D. was hit. No

drugs, no weapons, nothing. Not one joint. Not even a penknife. Like they were expecting something to go down."

"No sign of Linda either," Vik reminded her. "Wonder why she's disappeared? And Brick."

"That might be something we'd all like to know. Uniforms have checked out friends and relatives, but maybe I'll talk to her parents."

She began reading her notes. "And we still need a make on that Avon lady Mrs. Banks told me about."

"You want to place your Christmas order early?"

For once Vik wasn't being sarcastic. He was just tired.

"Marti, we've canvassed, shown pictures, nobody's seen nothin' and nobody's going to see anything, not in that neighborhood."

"Nobody's seen these photographs yet. Maybe someone will recognize one of these little girls."

"Marti, for crying out loud. Who in the hell you think's gonna give a damn about them? If we had a witness to anything, she's dead."

Ruth Price's niece was too busy to come here and make funeral arrangements. There was no service. The old woman had been cremated and her ashes sent to a local cemetery where nobody would ever visit her remains. She hadn't even been buried with her husband. Marti wondered if anyone had said Kaddish.

"Isaac gave a damn," Marti said. "We're going back. With these pictures."

They returned to the ravine where Danny Jones had been found. Isaac was sitting on his back steps and nodding in the warmth of the sun. She showed him the pictures.

"If I hear anything . . ." he promised again. For a moment he had a puzzled expression on his face. "Isaac don't never see nothin'."

"Listen, I need to know if the guy we found over there had anything to do with R.D. You hear something, let me know."

"Dare say R.D.'s not doing so good."

"No, he's not, but he'll live."

"Too bad." Isaac reached for his back pocket and she knew he was ready for another drink. She was going to have to line up a place for him to stay during the winter. The trick would be working out an arrangement that was acceptable to him.

Their next stop was the neighborhood surrounding the pool hall. They talked with four seven- or eight-year-old boys roller-skating nearby, and one did remember seeing Danny hanging around, but that was all.

Vik didn't say I told you so. He was as disappointed as Marti that they hadn't turned up anything.

Linda's mother lived on the north side of town. Marti and Vik parked in front of a large, ranch-style house. The yard was landscaped with evergreens and shrubbery. A Cadillac was parked in the driveway in front of an open garage door. No way Linda could blame her career choice on poverty.

Her mother, Mrs. Lyman, was a short, heavyset woman. She wore what appeared to be a wig clipped in short, feathery curls, and oversized glasses that had gone out of style. Instead of asking them in, she came outside and motioned them to a deck on the side of the house. The expression on her dark face was as sour as Vik's.

"I refuse to get involved with any of this mess with Linda. Haven't seen her in four years. Don't ever want to see her again."

They sat in webbed lawn chairs, shaded by a large oak tree.

"Then you haven't seen her in the past few days?" Marti said. "Do you know of anyplace where she might go?"

"Hah. Girl ain't got no friends. Too fast to make friends. Got two older sisters, both been to college. But not that one, not her. Brother went into the army. All of 'em makin' somethin' of themselves. All but her. Just like her daddy, that one. Never going to amount to nothin'." She sat back with a sigh that sounded almost like satisfaction.

"Sure made a mistake when I married that dog Wesley

Fremond. First husband, John Lyman, my other children's father, died. Lot older than me he was, but a good man. Took up with that no-count Wesley Fremond like a fool and had that child. Worse mistake I ever made. Ain't worth nothin', neither of 'em. Gave that child everything, just like the others, and look how she repaid me, stealin' 'fore she was twelve, out there whorin' now. Whipped that girl 'til she couldn't walk and she still defied me."

"Would she go to her father?" Marti asked.

"That fool done damned near drank himself to death. He's in a VA hospital in St. Louis. Can't imagine Linda wanting to have no more to do with him than he's had to do with her."

Mrs. Lyman spent another fifteen minutes complaining without providing any useful information. Marti and Vik were both in a lousy mood when they got back to the precinct.

Vik tossed the packet of snapshots on his desk. "Looks like we've got the evening off."

And Joanna didn't even have a softball game. Then she remembered Theo's Cub Scout meeting. "Oh no," she grumbled. "Not tonight."

Vik looked at her, his wiry eyebrows arched, but he didn't ask any questions. He cracked his knuckles, echoing her frustration, then began to shred a newspaper.

"Hey! Leave that mess around, Jessenovik, and we'll have mice making nests in here again. You know how long it took us to catch those two last year."

Just as they were ready to pack it in for the day, Vik got a call from the desk sergeant. The photographic comparisons on the bit of right front fender taken at the fire scene were ready. Vik decided to take them home.

32

It was a little after five when Marti parked in front of Ben Walker's bungalow and watched as Theo and Mike, both wearing blue Cub Scout uniforms, lugged their sleeping bags up to the porch. She still didn't know what she was going to say at their den meeting. A film she'd seen on "stranger danger" came to mind. Or she could talk about street gangs and drugs.

Theo tugged at his bag, dragging it up the five steps. He seemed thinner, more fragile beside Mike, who was at least ten pounds overweight and hefted his sleeping bag over his shoulder. Mike let Theo struggle with his instead of helping him. That pleased her.

She had intended just to let Theo know she'd be on time for the meeting, but she should go inside, say hello to Ben. He had mentioned talking with her about the camping trip after the meeting. If she didn't go in it would look like she was avoiding him. She was, but she didn't want him to think so. Annoyed, she got out of the car.

She hesitated at the screen door, trying to decide whether to knock, ring the bell, or call out hello and go in. She could hear the boys' voices and pushed open the screen door, following them. As she entered the hallway, Ben came to a doorway at the opposite end.

"Hi," she said, determined not to peek into any of the rooms as she walked toward him. She did anyhow, just a glance, and got a quick impression of dainty mahogany tables, a mantel with photographs and rumpled covers thrown over a sofa and chairs.

She reached Mike's room first, saw the boys kneeling on the floor sorting through camping gear, and went in. As she entered the room, Ben called for Mike.

"Hi, Mrs. Mac," he said, heading for the kitchen. "Check out those neat utensil sets we got at the army-navy store."

She sat on the carpet beside Theo, seeing Johnny as she looked at the planes and angles of their son's face in profile. He focused intently on the utensils and whatever it was that kept them hooked together. She felt a familiar ache, remembering Johnny at nine. He had been two years older than she was, her brother Nathaniel's best friend. He and Nate would sit together much as Theo and Mike did, sorting marbles, choosing baseball cards.

"You really want to go on this trip, don't you?"

"It's going to be great. Ben says there's a ferry we can ride across a river on without getting out of the car."

"You went camping once before."

His shoulders tensed. For a minute he seemed to huddle inside himself. Then he reached for his backpack and pulled out three pinecones. "I brought these back."

"From that trip? With your dad?"

"Yes."

"Why are you packing them now?"

"I don't know. I just want to bring them."

She wasn't sure what to say, but she wanted to keep Theo talking. "Where did you find them?"

"Near the lake where me and Dad caught that fish. The little one that we threw back."

And he was taking them back to the woods. But why? To have some memory of Johnny along with him? She touched one. Another cryptic message that she couldn't interpret and Theo couldn't explain. She reached for him, and he leaned against her.

He was more muscular than he had been at the beginning of summer, solid and not as thin.

"I haven't been home much the past week or so."

"That's okay. But I'm glad you're coming to my meeting tonight. Can you tell them the good stuff you do? Homicide cops help people too."

They sat quietly for a few minutes. Then he looked up at her, dark eyes solemn. "Please, Ma, don't talk about guns."

"No guns." She kissed the top of his head.

Ben was in the kitchen, wearing a chef's apron with SMOKIN' FIREMAN in red letters on the bib. His five-o'clock shadow suggested that he was one of those men who had to shave twice a day. She liked the scratchy feel of half a day's beard against her face. The top of her head came to his nose.

"Take a load off your feet," he invited, waving a dish towel. "Stay for supper. Got a salmon on the grill that just came out of the lake this afternoon. Lemon and butter, a little onion, wrapped in foil." He grinned. "The boys want burgers, of course."

She accepted a Pepsi, and watched as he moved from the refrigerator to the table with the grace of a dancer. The fish sounded good, but she wasn't ready to commit herself to sticking around. She could hear the boys' laughter, Theo's deep and enthusiastic, something she hadn't heard in a long time at home.

"Real good friends, those two," Ben said, pulling a stool up to the table and opening a can of pop. "Odd match."

She agreed, but didn't say why she thought so. She didn't know what made Mike, who had been the class bully in third grade, and Theo, who had never been in a fight, take to each other. She suspected it was the one thing they did have in common, a deceased parent, and tried thinking of them as a self-help twosome. But Mike wasn't getting any thinner and Theo wasn't becoming any more talkative and she couldn't see how either boy was much help to the other.

Ben sipped his pop, didn't seem uncomfortable with their lack of conversation. He got up to check the grill, then went down to talk to the boys. "Watching 'National Geographic,' " he said when he came back. "Maybe they are good for each other."

So, he wondered about that too.

"Is it good?" she asked. "Their being together so much?"

"Beats me," Ben said. "I wonder sometimes. Think it's right, interfering? They don't get into any trouble together, seem to have a good time. At least it hasn't made things any worse."

For some reason she had assumed that Ben would be glad Mike had someone as nice as Theo for a friend, that she was the one who should be concerned about Mike's influence. "There haven't been any problems," she admitted.

"Mike's grades have gone up since they've been doing their homework together."

She heard Theo laugh again.

"I wonder what they talk about sometimes," Ben said. "If they talk about . . ." he hesitated. "I don't know what that's like for a kid. Worse than for an adult maybe, harder to understand." He shook his head. "Theo talk to you about it?"

"No."

"Mike neither. Never know for sure what he's thinking."

"I guess we wait and see," Marti said.

He smiled unexpectedly. "Thought for sure you'd know what was best for them, Theo at least."

"No. It gets hard to know what's best for me sometimes. I just muddle along like everyone else." This was the first time they'd done more than make polite conversation about Theo and Mike. "I'm not sure you ever 'get over it.' Sometimes, I worry about how they cope."

"About as well as we do, I suspect," Ben said.

"I was hoping they did better than that." Ben was easy to talk to.

"Mike was supposed to go with her to the store the day it happened. At the last minute the next-door neighbor called and asked if he could come over. I keep telling Mike that he couldn't have prevented the accident if he was in the car. He was only four. I'm not sure he believes me." He got up to check the food, spoke with his back to her. "I think that, if they do talk about it, I'm glad."

She watched him fussing with the salad, chopping scallions and tomatoes, grinding pepper. When Johnny was worried he cooked meals that required a lot of preparation. The night he died he made pansit and another Filipino dish with shredded cabbage and pork chopped into tiny pieces. He had been worried that night. If he had been depressed he would have eaten custard-filled, chocolate-covered doughnuts. Before he'd gone out he had printed a note on the board by the telephone: *Theo, be home at noon. We'll work on the airplane.* He could not have killed himself four hours later. He had planned to come home.

She looked up to see Ben sitting across from her. "Got an anniversary of some kind coming up, don't you?"

"Yeah," she admitted. "Johnny's birthday. Fortieth. We always made a big deal out of birthdays."

"I can't stand the anniversaries. Make sure I work that night. Volunteer, if I have to. I get the guilts for leaving Mike. But I just can't handle it yet."

She spoke very quietly. "Me neither."

33

At noon on Thursday, Marti went to the house where Ruth Price had been found dead the week before. For the first time in four days the temperature was below ninety. The weather seemed almost pleasant at eighty-two degrees. Thin layers of wispy clouds drifted lazily across a bright blue sky. It was a nice day for an elderly woman to take a walk to the park.

Marti stood at the door Ruth Price would have used, looking at the paint peeling from the side of the house. The knee-high grass of a week ago was only ankle high now. The dandelions had bent to the blade of the lawn mower and sprung up again, numerous and fat.

A bee buzzed near her head. She waved the insect away and checked her watch. Twelve-fifteen, the time Mrs. Banks, the upstairs neighbor, said Mrs. Price would have gone out. There were three possible routes. Marti decided on the one that would take her past the clinic and set out, walking at the pace she thought an old woman would walk. Vik was right—she would never have had time to do anything like this in Chicago.

As she walked to the corner, she could see the red-brick belfry of a nearby church. She turned north on Seneca, where there were a number of small businesses. The street wasn't crowded, and everyone seemed to have someplace to go.

The burned-out clinic was near the corner of Seneca and Second Avenue. Joe's Market was right next door. She circled both buildings, noting the Dumpster behind the store. Joe would put his bruised and wilting produce out at about five o'clock. She wondered who would get Ruth Price's portion and enjoy an orange tonight.

The last two blocks to the park were residential, all of the houses older, mostly wood framed and well cared for. Marigolds, salvia, and petunias grew in front of many houses. There were lilac bushes, green now, and rosebushes heavy with blossoms. A man in a straw hat looked up from his weeding and smiled. This would have been a safe and pleasant walk for Ruth Price. Marti was convinced this was the route the old woman would have taken.

She stopped near the old firehouse and looked across the street to Truman Park. Another ravine, like the one where Danny Jones was found, was gouged deep into the earth. Here there were shade trees and benches near the clover-and-dandelion-speckled slopes. As she watched, a young woman spread a blanket under a tree and passed sandwiches to four children.

A man sat on one of the benches, reading a newspaper held close to his face. A tidy little gray-haired woman sat on another bench, with the straps of a blue canvas shopping bag over her arm.

Marti crossed the street. There were no teenagers, no blaring radios or boisterous conversation. The chatter of the children seemed to blend with the rustle of leaves.

She went to the young woman first, a pixie-faced strawberry blonde she might have mistaken for the children's older sister if it weren't for the slight bulge of her stomach and droop of her breasts. Marti showed her Ruth Price's photograph.

"The licorice lady," the woman said. "Is she okay?"

Marti shook her head.

One of the two boys stopped eating his sandwich. "Where is she?" He seemed to be the oldest, six maybe.

The woman turned to him. "Finish your lunch."

"Is she okay?" he persisted.

"We'll talk in a minute," the woman promised, then turned to Marti. "It was her in the paper, wasn't it?"

Marti nodded.

"There wasn't a picture, but I knew her name was Ruth."

"Auntie Ruth," the boy said.

"She always had a little bag of Nibs, those licorice pieces. I don't let the kids have much candy, but I didn't want to hurt her feelings. She always sat with that woman over there." She indicated the elderly lady with the blue shopping bag.

Marti thanked her.

The woman clutched the handles of the bag as Marti approached. Marti took out her shield. "Police, ma'am. I need to talk with you about your friend Ruth Price."

The woman's face was very dark, her skin smooth except for crow's-feet and laugh lines. There was a yellow filminess to the whites of her eyes, and her dark pupils were cloudy.

"I'm Ruth's friend, Addie Liz. I know she's dead. My granddaughter read it in the newspaper and told me. No funeral yet. There going to be one?"

"A niece had her body cremated."

"It would have been nice to say good-bye."

"Were you close friends?"

"Poor Ruth. I didn't even know where she lived. We just came to the park when the weather was good and sat here getting some sun." She made little pleats in her cotton skirt, rubbing the creases with her thick, short fingernails. "Most days she'd walk back with me and watch a little television. I live just a block away."

"Tell me about her."

"Nothing much to tell. She was a widow woman, like me. Most of what we liked to talk about happened before you were born."

Addie Liz nodded toward the children. "Ruthie took a likin' to them. Mannerly children. Respectful toward older folk." She cleared her throat and looked away for a moment. When she turned to Marti again her eyes were moist. "We gave each other little things sometimes. I got twelve grands and they always bring me things I ain't got no use for—perfumes, soap, way too much lotion. I brought what I didn't need to Ruthie. She brought me little things too. Heavy wool socks that belonged to her husband. Lord, but my feet get cold sometimes, even in summer. Circulation's poor. Sometimes she brought me a flower she picked along the way."

The old woman fingered a cameo brooch pinned to the collar of her blouse. The gilt was coming off and specks of white plastic showed in the swirls of the setting. "Loved oranges, Ruthie did. I'd bring her one most every week unless my grand-daughter forgot to get it for me. Ruthie would sit here and eat that orange, juice running down her chin, fingers gettin' all sticky. Always said she was going to stop and pick up a couple on her way home but I was never sure she had the money, 'specially not late in the month when the Social Security runs out."

Addie Liz began rummaging through the canvas shopping bag. "I live just down the street there. The nursing home. They steal from you, not just the attendants, other folks living there too. I leave 'em the stuff I don't care about."

She took out a black lacquered box with dragons painted on the lid. "My grandson sent me this while he was in Vietnam. My Otis. His name is on that memorial they got for them that didn't come home." She took out something wrapped in Kleenex. "Ruthie gave me this the day she died."

A small brooch. "Real silver, she said, but I don't think so. That's not what makes it special. It was a gift, from a friend. But that ain't why you came here, is it? You think I might know something about how she died. Or why."

Marti nodded.

"If I thought I could help you any I would have called long before now."

"Did she tell you anything that happened, anything she saw during her walk home the week before?"

"The night of that fire?"

"Yes."

"Ruthie was worried about who she didn't see. She was expecting to see this pretty blond girl that night who comes to see the doctor once a month. But the girl don't come, least not while Ruthie was there. When Ruthie found out someone died, she got worried that it was her. Wasn't no picture of one of them girls in the paper. But Ruthie said she saw this other girl, the one who was in the alley the night of the fire, the black one with the painted hair. Blue it was. Ruthie had seen her there before. The girl told Ruthie it wasn't nobody she knew who had died."

Ruth Price had seen Linda. Marti was sure of it.

"Did she tell you anything else about the girl with the blue hair?"

"That when she had seen her there a couple of weeks before, her hair was green."

"Did she say this girl was alone when she saw her near the clinic the night of the fire?"

"Ruthie said she was running out the front door. Said she wasn't friendly like the pretty blond girl. Said that if she hadn't walked right up to her when she saw her on the street a couple of days later, she wouldn't have found out the pretty one didn't die in the fire. Ruthie, she don't talk to hardly nobody. That girl she was worried about must have been really nice."

Was that all Ruth had seen—Linda leaving the clinic? Linda hadn't been seen since she was released from jail on Tuesday. Did Linda know too much, also? Unless she had a good hiding place, the odds on finding her alive could be getting slim.

34

Less than an hour after she left Truman Park, Marti was in the interrogation room at the county jail again with Vik, Vernon Halloran, and his attorney. After four enlargements, the photograph of the white car's fender had picked up a minuscule dent. The lieutenant had agreed that they had probable cause to inspect Halloran's Ford Escort. An evidence tech had found a tiny nick in the paint consistent with what showed up on the photo.

Halloran had consulted with his attorney and was ready to talk.

"I did not set that fire," he began. "I did not."

Marti looked at his attorney, Evelyn Ruckers, a petite bespectacled woman she had seen before in court.

"My client has agreed to cooperate in the investigation of a felony." Ruckers gave Halloran a nod.

"I was parked there the night of the fire. I was waiting for my daughter Wendy, to arrive so that I could prevent her from entering the clinic to purchase birth control pills. I had learned from my wife that Wendy purchased the pills at the clinic once a month. That's all. Thank God a friend of her mother's was able to detain her. When I saw the fire at the upstairs windows, I knew she couldn't be in there. I didn't think anyone was in there. The doctor had left."

Marti wasn't certain that she believed him. "From where you were parked, you could see the front of the clinic, part of the alley between the buildings, and anything that happened at either corner, correct?"

"Yes."

"What time did you arrive?"

"Five minutes to six."

"What's the first thing you observed?"

"Doctor Edwards walking down the alley, away from the clinic, about five minutes after I got there. I could see him in that space between the buildings."

"He wasn't driving?" Marti asked.

"No."

"Then what?"

"Maybe ten minutes later, a gray Lincoln drove past, turned the corner, and I could see it going down the alley."

R.D.'s car.

Halloran had also seen Linda go out through the front door. That was puzzling; as far as Marti knew, the only person with a key was Teresa, and her key didn't fit the lock. Marti was disappointed. She had hoped for more. They talked it over with the lieutenant and agreed to release Halloran without charging him—for now.

As soon as Marti got back to her office, she pulled out a copy of the floor plan at the clinic. Then she got Carmen Rodriguez on the phone.

"Where did you keep your purse, Carmen?"

"In the hall closet. Mrs. Johnson doesn't want us going in her desk."

Marti checked the floor plan. The bathroom was next to the closet, accessible to anyone.

"Where did you keep your keys?"

"I don't know. In my jacket pocket maybe, or my purse if there was enough room. It sort of depended, I guess."

That was probably true of Teresa, too. The position of the receptionist's desk did not provide a view of the hall. Anyone would have had access to their keys. The doctor's office was across from the bathroom, the examining room next to his office. Edwards himself could have taken the keys.

"Damn."

She looked up to see Halloran, his attorney, his wife, and Wendy coming into the room.

Wendy was a taller, more vibrant version of her mother with cornflower blue eyes, and thick blond hair.

"Wendy would like to ask you something," Evelyn Ruckers said.

"It's about the old lady I used to see in the alley," Wendy said. "I wanted to give her a sweater last week, but I didn't know where she lived, so I took it to Joe. He said she's the lady who got killed. I felt real bad. She always seemed like she was almost afraid of people. I just kept saying hello until she said hello back. I brought her some gloves once. It was so awful, the way she had to pick through the garbage."

"Her neighbor said she hardly ever spoke to anyone," Marti said. "But she did like well-mannered young people. I think she took the trouble to make sure that you were not one of the girls who died in the fire."

Wendy seemed pleased. For a moment, Marti felt good too, knowing that someone had noticed Ruth Price, had taken the time to speak to her and been persistent enough to get a response.

Marti didn't tell Wendy that by being concerned, Ruth Price might have called enough attention to herself to make someone want her dead.

"Takes after her grandfather," Vik said, when the Hallorans were gone.

Marti was surprised to see that it was only a few minutes past four.

"Has Edwards been released?" she asked.

Vik grunted.

"We can't question him without permission from his attorney, but I'd like to talk with Mrs. Johnson. Get a better feel for the routine at the other clinic. Those keys are bothering the hell out of me. Let's just drive by the clinic. She should be there until six."

Before they could leave, Slim and Cowboy came in.

"Brought someone in to see you," Cowboy drawled.

"Glodine," Slim said. He wasn't smiling or being flirtatious. They'd have a hard time forgetting that baby dolls had been passing through Lincoln Prairie and they hadn't picked up on it. If Glodine told Marti anything useful, that would help.

She went to the interrogation room. Glodine was jiggling her leg at a frantic pace. She hunched forward, alternately hugging herself and rubbing her arms.

Marti recognized the symptoms. "What are you coming down from?"

"Heroin."

And R.D., her dealer, was hospitalized. She must be cut off from her source. "Why'd you come here?"

"Might have something you want."

"Such as?"

Glodine began pacing. Her nose was running. She wiped it with a small, damp lump of tissue. "Called you about that clinic fire."

So, she was their anonymous tipster. "R.D. isn't the arsonist."

"He brought them little girls here. His fault Janey died. Gave you her ring. Used his key to his mother's house to get some of his papers." Glodine sat down again. "Can I smoke in here?"

"Not anymore."

"Can't smoke nowhere no more." Her leg began twitching again. She sniffled.

Marti gave her a Kleenex. "What do you want?"

"Need to get clean."

"Ever get clean before?"

Glodine shook her head. "Never wanted to."

"Easier things."

"I used to think so."

Marti tried to decide why any man would pay to have sex with Glodine. She was so scrawny the bones in her upper chest and shoulders showed through the T-shirt she was wearing. An army of blackheads had erupted on her forehead. She was bow-legged, and when she walked one of her feet turned in.

"You want to get clean or just get away from here? Where you from?"

"Kansas. Ain't never going back there." Glodine sniffled. "Ain't nothing in Kansas but hard times." She looked about the room. "Hell, ain't nothin' nowhere but hard times." She stood up, sat down, rubbed her jeans. "I got to get out of this. Out of all of this. He bring them little girls into this like he brought me, but hustling for a man don't seem so bad five, six years ago. Different now. Better off working for yourself."

She began pacing again. "Them babies was sold like they was nothing. Sold. I ask him how he be selling 'em? Ain't like he was fencing VCRs—they's somebody's children. He had Brick whip up on me, just for asking. Ain't right what he's doin'. Just ain't right."

She stood still, facing the wall. "I was helping him," she whispered, her voice so low Marti could just make out what she was saying. "I was helping him. I wouldn't put my little sisters on the street, but I was helping him." She turned to Marti. "You see why I gotta get offa this? Ain't right. Ain't none of it right. And I ain't been able to stay high enough to make it seem right. I get clean, now, or I die."

Marti took the envelope of photographs out of her purse. "You recognize any of these little girls?"

Glodine picked out four, but only knew them by the names R.D. gave them. "He kept 'em for himself a few days. Got hooked up with these perverts who make movies of 'em. Know what they do with them movies? Besides getting off, I mean? Show 'em to other kids. Here, we gonna do this. You gonna like it just like this little girl do. We gonna do what me an' your momma do.

See. Just like this." She shuddered. "Sick, rotten bastards. All of 'em."

"You know where any of these girls are now?"

"Can't say, but I can tell you where they might be."

Glodine gave her addresses in Milwaukee, St. Louis, and Minneapolis.

"Don't mean they still there, though. Don't even mean that's where they went."

"How many little girls were there?"

"Not many. Just one every month or so at first. Then it got to be more like one every coupl'a weeks. Seemed that way, at least. Only the pretty little light-skinned ones went to Antioch. He'd keep 'em here when they wasn't filming. Wasn't for much more than a week. Some of 'em, they ain't never done nothin' like this before. They be scared, shamed. He don't care."

"How long has R.D. been doing this?"

"Year or so, I guess. He always liked to have something real young every once in a while. Wasn't till he got hooked up with them folks in Antioch that he started doin' it regular."

"Why did they go to Dr. Edwards?"

Glodine looked at her, aware of the implications. "Can't testify. Not against the doctor. Not against R.D. Not unless you get me outta here."

"Why?" Marti repeated.

"Make sure they ain't got no diseases. Get rid of the babies if they knocked up. I was pregnant when I come here. Sure can't tell my momma. She wanting me to be the first to finish school." She closed her eyes. "Look, this wasn't no two-bit operation. Plenty of money in it for R.D. and everybody else. Anybody got AIDS or VD, R.D. be outta business. And maybe in big trouble, too."

Marti looked at the girls in the pictures. She wasn't sure she wanted to know what had happened to any of them.

35

Marti let Slim and Cowboy know what she had found out from Glodine. She called in a favor and made arrangements to get Glodine into a drug rehab program right away. Then she put in a call to Denise Stevens and arranged to meet her at the hospital that afternoon to talk with Christina.

When she told Vik about Glodine he almost smiled. "I like it when they get even."

"Being crippled isn't enough," she said. "R.D. was responsible for bringing Janey here. He's responsible for her death. Everyone that child came into contact with contributed to the abuse. And what about Edwards? Maybe you can't expect much from a pimp, but a doctor is supposed to heal, not harm."

She remembered Mrs. Johnson. There was still enough time to get to the clinic before six o'clock.

As they left the precinct, she picked up a copy of the afternoon *News-Times*. The headline read, DOCTOR RELEASED IN ARSON INVESTIGATION. The artist's sketch of Janey Willis and a shot of Edwards entering the precinct were also on the front page. She scanned the article. Edwards was questioned about the fire and released. No mention of the prescription-drug offenses, and the reporter wouldn't have been aware of the insurance fraud when the story went to press. It acknowledged that the dead girl's identity was known without revealing her name. There was no mention of Teresa Martinez.

When Marti and Vik got to the clinic, Edwards's BMW was parked outside. Vik went in first, down the narrow, dark hallway.

He barged into the reception area and stopped abruptly, motioning Marti with one hand to stay back. She stopped, listening. Didn't hear anything. Vik didn't speak. She tested the floor for creaks as she took several steps back, within hearing distance but farther out of sight. She could see Vik in the doorway, not moving. She unholstered her weapon, hand tight on the grips, and flattened herself against the wall so she could cover the front door and Vik. She felt a vein pulse in her forehead and a familiar tightening in her stomach as she waited.

"You!" a man spoke. Not the doctor's voice. "You let him go!" Hispanic accent. Angry. She recognized the voice now. "He kills my sister and you do not arrest him. And only this other girl is important, this girl they do not even call by name. My Teresita who is always so good, it is as if she never existed at all."

Weapon. He had to have one. Holding the doctor hostage? Vik was immobile. She watched his hand and waited with a bitter taste in her mouth.

"Listen, son, the person who did this will not get away." Vik's voice was quiet, his tone soothing. "Right now, I need to help you."

"You lie so I will not kill him, but I will. I will shoot him just like I shot that pimp you let get away. My Teresita is dead and these men are allowed to go free."

"Look, Martinez," Vik made a small backward movement with his hand. He wanted her to go outside, find another way in. She'd have to trust him to know the best way to proceed. He knew where everyone was in the room, what was happening.

"You're upset," Vik said. "Any man would be, losing his sister like that. I'm here to help you."

Marti began moving toward the door. Noise? She didn't think so. Vik would be alone as soon as she stepped outside. Where were the windows? She listened to her heart pumping. Took a deep breath. One in the reception room, south side. Vik's signal better mean Martinez would have his back to her.

"I don't think you really want to be in this situation, Martinez. I think the two of us can work this out."

She gripped the doorknob. Waited.

"Just take a minute and think. I know you're upset about this. But things are still okay here. We don't have a problem yet that we can't work out."

As Vik spoke, Marti turned the knob. The click sounded as loud as a gunshot.

"I know how hard everything's been on you, but we can still work this out."

Hot air rushed at her. Sunlight hit her in the eyes. Martinez had better not see it. Squeezing outside, she pushed the door to the jamb slowly until she heard a click, softer now. She went to the window. Open halfway, covered by burglar bars. Vik in profile, still talking. "I know you don't want anyone to get hurt here. Let's just work this out."

The doctor was sitting on a stool beside a cardboard box and a stack of files. Martinez was standing behind the receptionist's desk, his back to Marti. She trained her weapon on him, concentrating so she would know when he was ready to shoot before he got a chance to pull the trigger. His shoulders would tense. She wished she could look into his eyes. The eyes always telegraphed it first when they made up their mind to shoot.

"Now listen, son, just do what I say and nobody will get hurt." Vik couldn't turn toward the window to be sure she was there without giving her position away. He was assuming she'd caught his signal and had enough time to position herself. Good.

"Why should I trust you?" Martinez stood with his legs apart, still ready to shoot. "You have betrayed my sister, letting these men go."

"Son, your sister wouldn't want you to do this. Who takes care of your mother if anything happens to you? You're the man of the house now. Your father would want you to take care of the women. Let us take care of the killer."

"My father would want my sister avenged."

"Son, you've got to put that gun down. Hold your hands out, both of them, then drop the gun on the floor."

"No." He shook his head, looking away from Vik for a moment, uncertain. "No." More insistent. "No! You let that pimp go free. You let this one go free. You arrest no one. They kill my sister and go free."

The sun was beating hot on Marti's back, sweat soaking through her blouse. Vik hadn't talked him down yet, but he had taken control. She tightened her hold on the grip. She had a clear shot.

"Listen to me, Martinez. My partner is right outside the window, gun drawn, ready to shoot."

"You try to trick me again." Voice louder, getting agitated now. Gun waving, not aimed at anyone.

She waited. Martinez, shoulders heaving, arms steady again, was getting calmer.

"Son, cops don't travel alone. My partner's behind you. Listen."

Martinez stiffened. His head turned just a little.

She spoke. "Put both arms out in front of you. Slowly. Drop the gun on the floor. Do it now."

He froze. Then his arms came up.

"Slow," she ordered.

He complied.

She heard a thump.

"Now put your hands on your head."

As soon as Vik had Martinez's weapon and his own gun unholstered, she ran back into the building.

After two uniforms had taken Martinez away, Dr. Edwards remained sitting on the stool by the file cabinet. He had given a brief description of Martinez coming in, drawing the weapon, threatening to kill him. When asked a question requiring only a yes or no answer, that was all he provided. He remained subdued, impassive, almost as if it had happened to somebody else.

Marti thought of the photographs of the girls. Would he react?

"Recognize anyone?" she asked, taking them out of the envelope.

Edwards looked at the top picture for a long time. His fingers curled into fists. She watched, taken by surprise when he slapped the flat of his hand against the file cabinet.

"That bitch." His voice was raspy. "She gave you those."

He looked at her, his eyes dark and bright with anger. "She stole my keys, went into my house when I wasn't there. My house. Thawed out a steak and cooked it in my kitchen. Went into my wine cellar and drank from an eight-hundred-dollar bottle of wine and poured a dozen more on the floor. Broke into the cabinet and threw thousands of dollars' worth of china against the wall. Helped herself to my wife's negligees. Plugged the toilet with my underwear." His hands began to tremble and his shoulders shook. "She invaded my home. That whore invaded my home. Said she could do any damned thing she pleased."

Now Marti knew whom he meant.

"That bitch," he said. "And that bastard R.D. laughed in my face when I told him. Said he might come with her next time. Asked me what was I going to do—call the cops?"

Linda and R.D. had realized the position Edwards was in because of the baby dolls. And they all had realized how little power he had when he did nothing about the break-in.

"Linda, that whoring bitch! She was supposed to die that night!" He stood up, picked up a metal tape dispenser, and threw it across the room. Glass exploded as it hit the window.

Edwards stared at the damage and clenched his fists until his knuckles were pale. He was breathing hard. An angry crime, arson, and now she had an angry man.

His car, Marti thought. Where was his car the night of the fire? Halloran said he saw the doctor walking down the alley. Edwards had said he was in his car. But someone would have noticed the car one way or the other.

36

After Marti and Vik left the clinic, she called the lieutenant. Dirkowitz agreed to send out three teams immediately to determine where the car had been parked and if anyone else had seen Edwards walking. Then Marti drove them to Howie's Take-out, where they ordered six hot dogs, fries, and two large Cokes, and headed for the lake. Vik looked exhausted. She felt the same way. She could smell her own sweat. Acrid, scared sweat. Vik smelled of it too. She knew that any officer who came out of a hostage situation should take the rest of the day off, minimum, but they still had too much to do.

Lake Michigan was a placid blue. Waves broke gently along the shore, and in the distance dozens of sails dipped and skimmed across the horizon. Strings of red and blue markers identified the swimming areas. As calm as the lake seemed, the currents could be swift and fierce.

Instead of heading for the sand they stayed in the park among the pines, and found a picnic table not far from the inlet where the yachts and small craft passed through to reach the slips in the harbor. They both looked out at the water. "We'll find out more when we locate Linda," Vik said.

"She isn't making it easy."

"Bet anything she and Brick are somewhere in Chicago. I don't think they'll go too far from home. Easier to hide in a place you're familiar with."

He unwrapped a hot dog. "That gun wasn't big enough to kill anybody. Martinez could have shot point-blank into the doctor's head without causing brain damage. Nice what he did to R.D., but I don't want anything bad to happen to Edwards until after he's behind bars." He stuck a straw through the cup lid and took a long swallow. "Nice job, covering me."

"Thank God you went charging ahead. Could have gotten out of hand if we were both in there. You did a good job of talking him down."

"My dad came up on something like that once. Guy was alone, though. Barricade. Dad said he talked to him the way he would talk to me, but if one of my kids pulled a stunt like that . . ."

Marti smiled.

"So, when's the camping trip?" he asked.

"They're leaving tonight."

She squeezed ketchup out of a plastic packet onto a napkin and dunked a few fries in it. "If there's not too much going on around here on Saturday, I'm going to Chicago for a couple of hours."

Vik swallowed a mouthful of hot dog, washed it down with some pop. "I thought there might be something special coming up."

"Birthday," she said. "He would have been forty."

Reaching over, Vik covered her hand with his.

On their way back to the precinct, they swung by the ravine where Danny Jones's body had been found, just a few blocks from the lake. Parking near the compression bridge that spanned the ravine, they walked along the gravel shoulder, looking down at the undergrowth that marked the descent to the narrow stream of water.

"Some river," she said.

"It used to scare me," Vik said. "Looking down there when I was a kid. This was downtown. The equivalent to a mall now, I suppose. We'd buy school clothes at the Globe, buy shoes at Hein's, stop at Druces or the Rexall drugstore for the best ice cream sodas in town, or go to Kilbanes for lunch. We might even go to a movie. Blumberg's furniture store used to be right across the street. Me and Mildred bought our bedroom set there. Still got it. Store's gone. Most all of it's gone now. Busy place back then."

"Too bad it's not busy now," she said. "Busy enough to have a few witnesses, anyway."

Vik shook his head. "Colder this case gets, the more it looks like it'll end up in the open file. I don't like cases like that."

"His composite ran in the newspaper yesterday. They're running it on Sunday too. Maybe we'll get something from that. He had to have a reason to come here when he got out of jail."

As they left she saw Isaac dozing on the steps. She wasn't sure she wanted to wake him, but the puzzled expression he had had the last time she was here nagged at her. What if she wasn't asking the right questions? What if he was withholding some tidbit of information until she did? She hesitated, then veered toward Isaac, letting Vik walk to the car. No sense mentioning anything to Vik that would sound like a hunch. He'd never let her forget it.

"Isaac! Wake up!"

"Huh? What? Oh, Officer Mac."

He sat up, rubbing his eyes, then reached for the half-empty bottle hidden behind his back and smiled.

"You back here again? The boy what died over there's worrying you, ain't it?"

"Sure is," she said.

"Wasn't nothin' but an ordinary stranger. Wasn't from around here. No need for you to bother with it so."

"Someone killed him."

"Yeah, well." He got that look again.

"You remember something you're not telling me?"

"No, ma'am."

"Tell me what you heard again."

He repeated the story, sound effects and all.

"What happened before that?"

"Nothin'." He paused. "Long time before that some kids riding around the parking lot on skateboards."

"Did anything happen the night after that didn't happen that night?"

"Noisier. Cops still there, keepin' folks away."

"What about the night before?"

"Someone come through here whistlin'." Isaac whistled a song she couldn't identify. He was halfway through a second rendition when he stopped. "Woman come through here. She change the way she walk."

Marti had no idea what he meant.

"Sure it was a woman, not a kid?"

"Yup. Walked like she goin' over there, by the bridge. Stones go to crunchin'. She stop by the ravine, stop whistlin'. Whistle again when she get to the sidewalk."

Denise Stevens met Marti at the hospital in a red straw hat with a nosegay of white silk carnations attached to the brim. Marti filled her in on what Glodine had told her and gave her the addresses. Denise already had a set of the photographs. They sat in a waiting area near the front of the hospital.

"I can't make you any promises on this," Denise told her. "I can get the local departments to investigate. Do you want to know if I get any information on the girls?"

"Probably not, but tell me anyway, so I can feel depressed and inadequate for a few days. How's Christina?"

"Coming around. We've had a few conversations. I think she's ready to talk to you. I've talked with her mother a few more times, too. She got herself locked up for manslaughter when Christina was three. Christina's been in foster care since her mother went to jail."

"Why didn't the mother get her back?"

"Couldn't at first. Had to get a job, place to live, the usual. By then Christina had gone through half a dozen foster homes, was in a class for behavior-disordered children. She was seeing a school psychologist who advised against her being returned to her mother. The mother didn't fight it too hard. Didn't know how. Christina got worse, but interestingly enough, found foster parents who were willing to keep her—insisted on it."

"Which one of them was abusing her?"

"I get the impression she was kind of like a pet, got passed around among the foster father's friends."

Marti felt a familiar churning in her stomach. "I hate working with kids. It hurts my ears to hear this. How do you do it?"

"I have to."

That seemed like an odd thing to say, but Marti didn't pursue it. "Her mother said she doesn't want her?"

"Her mother has heard all these stories about what a rotten human being Christina is. She's scared to death of taking her on. I went to Reverend Douglas, he contacted a church near where the mother lives, and we've got some church sisters working on it. I think that if we can set up the right network for them, provide them with resources, we might be able to get them together."

"Who did the mother kill?"

"One of her classmates. Over Christina's father. She was sixteen. She's finished school now, drives a bus for the city, bought herself a small house. No other kids."

Marti wondered which foster parent had called Christina a narrow-assed hussy. "I hope you can work something out, Denise, but I don't believe in miracles anymore." She thought of the time it must have taken to accomplish this much. "Nobody else would have taken it this far. You deserve to get lucky."

"I'm not the only one who cares about her. If she does talk to you, it'll be because you didn't assume she stole that teddy bear. You see something worth salvaging too."

"I see how difficult the salvage job will be."

"Maybe, but not impossible."

They headed for the elevator.

Christina was still in her room, but this time she was dressed in jeans and a loose-fitting blouse. Her hair was braided and fastened with puppy-dog barrettes. She didn't smile when they came in, but Marti got the impression that she was glad to have company. She hid a book she had been writing in, but not before Marti was able to see that it was a connect-the-dots game.

Denise spoke first. "Did you get down to the rec room today?"

Christina shook her head.

"They've got a movie tonight. The lights will be low, you won't have to talk with anyone, and you won't have to be by yourself. Give it a try."

Christina remained noncommittal.

"It'll be easier once you're back to doing the things most twelve-year-olds are doing. It'll seem strange being a kid for a while, but I've got a few other kids I can introduce you to who will help you along."

"Where do I go when I leave here?"

"I'm still working on it. Where do you want to go?"

"Rather be in one of them group homes. Ain't going to no foster home no more. Run away again before I'll stay there."

"Running away isn't always bad," Denise told her. "Means you don't like where you are, and sometimes you shouldn't. But at your age it can get you into worse trouble. So you just stay put here until I can work something out. About time you did what was good for Christina, like telling Officer Mac how you got here."

"Linda," Christina said. "She bring me to her place. Tell me she in the movies, I can be too. Tell me I can make money." She began twisting her braid. "I knew what she was really talkin' about. Hard to imagine her a real movie star. It wasn't nothin' I couldn't handle, though. They wasn't the first."

Marti didn't ask who the first was. She didn't want to know. "Where did you meet Linda?"

"At the bus station. She take me to her apartment. Real nice place. R.D. come. I know what's goin' down 'fore I got there. It's okay. They weird out there at that house where they make them movies but I figure you gotta get used to it. Linda got some pills she give you, you don't much care what they do."

Marti unclenched her fists and took out the photographs. "You ever see any of these girls?"

"Ain't nobody around what's my age but me." She looked anyway. "No."

"Did you want to leave the apartment or either house at any time?" Marti asked, hoping to establish the felonies.

"Where would I go?"

"Did you want to leave?" Marti asked.

"Didn't want to do them movies."

"Did Linda explain what you would do in the movies?"

"Asked me who I'd been with. I tol' her just my foster father and his friends. She said I'd get paid for it now. Lied about that."

"How did you get to the house where you were filmed?"

"R.D. Brick was in the car, and Linda, but R.D., he like to drive."

"Did you want to have sex with any of those men?"

"Who would ever want to? But it wasn't that bad," Christina said. "I didn't know any of them but R.D. I liked not havin' to see them again."

Marti had no idea what to say to her. MacTavish was propped up on a pillow on the bed. She picked him up. "Know who gave you this?"

"Had to be Glodine." For the first time, Christina's voice broke. She looked out the window, blinking fast. "She say I shouldn't do this. That I should be in school. She know I don't want to go back to that house no more and make no more movies. She help me when I come back here 'cause they hurt me."

Marti handed Christina the teddy bear. Tears streamed down the young girl's face as she hugged him, but she didn't make a sound.

Marti's beeper went off before she left the hospital. A relative had come in to identify Danny Jones.

"Feast or famine," she said to Denise, but she was eager to talk with whoever it was.

A young man close to Jones's age was waiting in the squad room, wearing a business suit and a blue tie with little red and white hexagons. Vik handed Marti a form. He'd asked a few routine questions, but was waiting for her.

The young man didn't seem upset about having to identify the body, and he wasn't fidgety or nervous. As she sat down, he took another sip of coffee and looked at her, waiting.

She glanced at Vik's notes. "Michael Jamison. How are you related to Danny Jones?"

"We're cousins. A friend of my mother's saw the picture in the paper and called to see if it was anyone in the family. My mother was reluctant to get involved."

"How well did you know him?"

"Didn't, really. You know how it is. Some people stay in the south, some move north. My mother came here when she was in grade school. Made arrangements through someone in a church back there to live with a family here."

"How was your mother related to Danny?"

"He was her younger sister's child, but they hadn't seen each other since she came here. He and I never met, but my mother has pictures. Danny looked just like one of my uncles."

"Did anyone ever hear from Danny?"

"Oh, he called when his parents died. Car crash. My mother thought he wanted to come here with Virgie, but Momma, well, she didn't want to take on the responsibility."

That should have been something his mother would understand. Someone had taken her in. Giving back was an old custom, an obligation, years ago. Too many had forgotten it.

"Who's Virgie?"

"Danny's little sister, Virginia."

"How old?"

"Eleven, twelve maybe."

She got out the list of names and the pictures, showed him the snapshots.

He shook his head. "We've got a picture of both of them on the mantel. She's not here. Why would she be?"

Instead of answering, Marti scanned the list of names. Jeannie was as close as she came.

"Do you have any idea why he was here?"

"My mother says that Virgie called her from Kentucky, said he was in jail, that she didn't have any place to stay. Momma said she could come til he got out. Then Virgie called back, said she was here but she had met up with a friend she'd be staying with. When Mom didn't hear anything else, she figured everything must be okay. When Danny called she told him the same thing."

And now Danny was dead and there was no trace of his younger sister.

By the time Marti got home a little after seven, she was so tired she didn't even feel hungry. She went into the kitchen and sat in the Boston rocker near the window and thought about getting up to make a sandwich. The house was quiet. Sharon and Lisa were at choir practice, Joanna had a softball game, and Theo had left for Wisconsin. Bigfoot, their "Heinz Fifty-seven" mongrel, padded into the room. He was the size of a St. Bernard, mostly tan with random white markings. Johnny had picked him out at the pound seven years ago and named him for his feet, which had been totally out of proportion with his body when he was a pup. He pushed at her hand with his nose.

"Lonesome?" she asked. "Your buddy took off without you."

He nuzzled her hand, sighing as she stroked between his ears. Then he slumped at her feet.

She leaned back against the cushion and was beginning to doze when Joanna came in.

"Win?" she asked.

"By a run. Bottom of the seventh." Joanna swung her long auburn braid behind her. Her uniform pants were streaked with dirt. She had slid into the plate more than once.

"Sorry I wasn't there."

"That's okay."

From the sound of Joanna's voice she wasn't sure.

Within a few minutes Joanna had set up a tray table beside her, brought over two glasses of iced tea and sandwiches made with cold chicken breasts.

"You look beat, Ma. Do you have to go back out?"

"No."

Joanna sat at the table, not far from the rocker.

Marti thought about the party last Saturday night, wondered if she wanted to mention Joanna's early departure. "Things okay with you?"

"Ma, I left the party early because I was tired."

Marti didn't have enough energy for a serious discussion. "Hard to imagine you being too tired to dance."

"Well, going to dances and parties is not what I thought it would be. Mostly, it's boring. You want some chamomile tea? It'll help you relax, get to sleep."

Sharon said kids sometimes used the word *boring* to describe depression. She decided to get up, but it took her several minutes to summon the energy. She went over to Joanna, stood behind her. Joanna leaned her head against her and closed her eyes.

"You're tired, too."

"I guess so."

"Why are dancing and partying so boring?"

Joanna didn't speak, didn't move away. Marti felt her tension, began kneading her shoulders. "I don't think you were bored. Don't think you were shy or tired, either. I remember a little girl who wanted to be a ballerina and did pirouettes for her daddy. Break his heart if you didn't dance no more."

"I can't break his heart," Joanna whispered. "Dad's not here anymore."

Marti sat down, pulled Joanna toward her, felt Joanna's hair soft against her lips as she spoke. "I don't know when it stops hurting."

Joanna's shoulders began to shake. She cried in gulping sobs. Marti rocked her, feeling her own tears warm on her face.

37

The first thing Marti thought of when she woke up Friday morning was Isaac and the "woman who changed the way she walked." What if Isaac had seen something? What if he translated that to something he could hear? Two blocks from the precinct an idea occurred to her. As soon as roll call was over she went to see Mrs. Banks.

The old woman was sweeping the front steps when Marti got there. Sweat glistened on her dark face from the exertion. She hitched up three or four slips that hung below her loose-fitting shift. "You find out who did it?"

"Not yet."

"Poor Ruthie. That niece of hers didn't even come bury her." She made chewing movements. "They came from the church and put them locks in just like you said. You sure they ain't kept a key?"

"Real sure."

"Don't want to wake up one night dead in my bed."

Marti tried not to smile. "I need you to look at these pictures, tell me if there's anyone you could have seen around here who changed the way she looks in the photograph."

"You want me to look at these pictures and say that's the one, but she didn't look nothing like that when I saw her?"

"Exactly."

"Chile, I ain't never heard of nothin' like that before. How I gonna be doing that?"

But she took the pictures. Sitting on the top step, she studied them for a while. Then she put them down and looked up and down the street. "Childrens ain't out yet. Be quiet for another half hour." She looked at the pictures again. "If this one had long hair, maybe."

Marti took a marker with ink that could be wiped off out of her purse and made the change.

"That's that girl who spent half the day wandering the neighborhood."

"Which day?"

"The Tuesday before Ruthie died."

"Was she the Avon lady, too?"

"Didn't open my door to that fool Avon lady. 'Sides, that was Wednesday."

"Did this girl see you?"

" 'Course not. I got these binoculars I look through. Got to keep folks like that from around here. She either looking to pick up someone or deal some drugs. I call that hot line and report 'em. I was waiting for her to do something, so I could report her, but she was jus' walking the streets. Every so often she'd walk past."

R.D. had driven through the alley behind the clinic a little after six, just about the time Ruth Price would have been there. But Ruth never mentioned any of that to Addie Liz. Either nothing happened to catch her attention or, because she had seen Linda there before, her presence didn't seem unusual.

"You're sure that this is the person you saw?"

"Saw her up close enough to know. Them's real good binoculars. She was chewing gum."

"Did Ruthie see her?"

"Ruthie go to the store and get the newspaper about the time the girl leave. Can't say as I saw them talking."

That must have been when Ruth Price asked about Wendy Halloran. Back at the precinct, Marti showed Vik the altered photograph of Linda. "She's got to be somewhere, alive or dead."

"Ready for my news?" Vik asked. "The doctor's car was

parked three blocks from the clinic all evening. Joe saw him walk to and from the clinic right about the time the fire started."

"We got him?" she said. "We got him!"

"Premeditated," Vik said. "Wanted Linda, it looks like he decided he might as well get Teresa too. He might not have known Janey was there."

"Because Linda broke into his home," Marti said. "The one place where we all want to be safe." Edwards had become a victim. He had felt violated and powerless just as all victims do, and then Linda and R.D. had told him they could make him feel that way at will. And he'd believed them.

Marti pulled out everything she had on Danny Jones. The files were slim. This was the one crime that she couldn't associate with anything else—the one she didn't think they were going to solve.

"Jones had that two-day-old bruise on his face," she reminded Vik. "Six months from now they'll pick up a drunk, or a junkie, or someone trying to walk on a breaking and entering. They'll either remember that Jones got into a fight with someone or confess to running him down after they brooded over losing a fight with him."

Vik's phone rang while she was talking.

"Guess what?" he said, when he hung up. "Got a warrant on Preppy. California wants him for running a porn shop there three years ago. Man moves around. They traced him to Atlanta first, then here. He changes his name a lot, too. He was Bruce Derrick in Atlanta, Bobby Dann in L.A., and now he's Bill Demming."

"And out on bail," Marti said. "He could be in Switzerland by now. I'm sure Demming had enough contacts to hop a jet out of here."

Vik aimed a pencil at one of the calendars.

"Why don't we take a ride out to that place?" Marti suggested. "The warrant makes it legitimate. We need to think through this Jones homicide away from the office."

"We need a decent night's sleep and a weekend away from here," Vik grumbled. "Is this just a hunch?"

"Yes," she said. "So what?"

38

Linda twisted the dial again. Demming had written down the combination to the safe, but she couldn't get it to open. She pushed at the clothes that were still in the way. She hated being cooped up in a closet, even if the door was open. She'd been locked in closets when she was a kid, 'cause Momma knew she was scared of the dark. Didn't bother her none now, though. Wasn't nothing bothering her now. That was some good shit she found downstairs. Best hit she'd had in a long time.

She tried the combination again. Nothing. Demming, everything was his fault, all of it. Everything was fine until he came along. She might have to bring home a little girl for R.D. every once in a while, but not like she had to once he met Demming.

Little whores, all of them, none of them worth nothin'. She beat up on them every chance she got, and not just so's they'd be glad to see R.D. He got off standing outside the door and listening to 'em crying and begging anyway. He beat Glodine's ass too. Brick just grabbed Glodine by the neck so she'd pass out. R.D. whipped up on her.

Linda knew she had to get out of here when R.D. did that. He wasn't even anybody she knew anymore. He was like Momma. Nobody was ever going to beat up on her again.

She would have got away after she broke into the doctor's house if Edwards hadn't told R.D. Then she had to hand over the jewelry, make like she had been planning to surprise him. Good thing for her R.D. thought it was funny. Might have whipped up on her then.

She looked at the gun. Wouldn't nobody beat her no more. She wasn't taking another whipping from nobody. Best thing to happen from all of this. Forced her to look out for herself.

She thought of the girl. Virgie, she called herself. R.D. liked giving them new names. Called her Jeannie. He wanted to keep her. She told him the girl was too damned dumb to be of any use to him. And she was. Jeannie took every pill she left out for her that night. Killed her damned self, the girl did.

All of them were stupid. Jeannie's brother didn't have the brains God gave a turnip. Damned fool gonna tell her she'd better bring him his sister or he'd go to the cops. If she had known he was gonna run right into that car, she wouldn't have bothered going toward him so fast. Damned near went over that ravine.

She could still see his face, hear the thud. God, that was good. Damned fool actually trusted her. Folks did trust her. The little girls would come right home with her, no matter how crazy a story she told them. They believed her. That old woman walked right up to her too, wanting to know who had died in the fire. Might have taken a long time to find the old bag if she hadn't.

Linda tried the screwdriver again. There had to be something to unscrew. If Demming hadn't put the thing in the floor like this . . . Plenty of money in here, she was going all the way to California, get in some real porn flicks. Damn, if she could get at the whole safe she could find a way to get it open. At least she didn't have to worry about nobody catching her. Thinking about that made her laugh.

39

Marti communicated their destination to Dispatch after they were en route. They parked on the street and made their way to the house, keeping under the tall pines and avoiding the driveway. Newspapers were scattered on the steps near the front door, and the red and white geraniums, which had looked perky in their cedar planters the last time she was here, were dying in the hot sun.

The house had an empty look. Keeping away from the building, Marti circled around to the back, Vik behind her. No car in the garage. She followed a path farther into the dense shrubbery and found the car that had been used to kill Danny Jones parked in a clearing. The old man who owned it hadn't reported it missing. He probably didn't know it was gone. They walked back to the house, weapons drawn, staying away from the driveway.

As far as she could determine, if anyone was inside she and Vik had remained unobserved. She went to the door that led to the kitchen and peeked through the window where the ruffled curtain was tied back. A woman was lying on the floor. Marti could see her legs. She wasn't moving.

She made a fist and put it to her ear, so Vik would notify the Antioch force and request backup. Then she waited until he came back from the car. The door wasn't locked. They stepped inside and listened. No sound but the metallic tick of a clock amplified by the quiet. She went over to the woman. Mrs. Preppy had been shot to death.

Weapons drawn, they searched in silence. The swirling

texture of the plaster wall pressed against Marti's shoulders as she covered Vik. Sweat began trickling down the small of her back and was soaking her armpits.

Vik opened a door. Broom closet. Another, the laundry room. No basement. He followed her into the dining room, where everything was painted and upholstered in shades of pale blue. Marti watched as Vik searched among the clothes that hung in a deep closet near the front door. There was a sudden loud buzz. Vik whirled, taking aim. They followed the fly into the den, watched the insect land. Preppy was slumped over the desk. There were two entrance wounds in his back, and a faint odor in the room. Without touching him to check for rigor, Marti guessed he hadn't been dead more than seven or eight hours. Her mouth was dry. She wiped the palms of her hands on her slacks. They went back to the living room. If the killer was still in the house, he or she wasn't on the first floor.

Certain that there wouldn't be anyone at their backs, they went to the staircase. She tested the bottom step. No creak. They kept to the sides, Vik by the banister, Marti by the wall.

Upstairs, wood floors, polished, no creaking. Vik licked his lips and took a deep, quiet breath. They moved down the hall, searching room by room. The first had pink walls, rug, canopy, and bedspread. A little girl's room at a glance. Rope restraints were attached to the headboard near little stuffed animals that nestled on the pillows. An adult-size wolf costume was folded at the foot of the bed. A life-sized stuffed tiger bared its fangs, and a riding crop and whip had been tossed across its back. A VCR and a television were on a movable platform.

The next room was smaller, all chintz and maple, ruffled and feminine. Dolls filled a cradle and spilled out of a doll carriage. Half a dozen large ragdolls huddled in a corner, heads wobbly. Metal manacles dangled from all four corners of the four-poster twin bed. Marti had viewed porn films ten years ago with the same props. If she had thought about it, she would have expected something original.

Back in the hallway they came to the master bedroom. Marti thought she heard something and paused, ear to the door. She heard it again—indistinct, but human. She exhaled, steeled herself for what she might find in the room. At least someone in there was alive. She flattened herself against the wall next to the door. Reaching over, she turned the knob and eased the door open. Nothing happened. A distinct grunting noise grew a bit louder, and she heard a muttered curse.

Someone she couldn't see was gasping, panting, as if they were doing something that required a lot of exertion. Whoever it was had not observed the door opening.

She remained in the doorway, looked at Vik, who was covering her from behind, and shrugged. She couldn't tell who it was—male, female, nothing.

She had been in this room once before, with Mrs. Preppy. She peered inside now. The door to the walk-in closet was ajar. Someone was in there. All she could remember about it was pairs of shoes lined up and the three walls of clothing. She listened again, then raised a finger. One person. She was sure.

Marti motioned to Vik to stay back and stepped into the room. She tiptoed over to the partially open closet door.

Linda, on her knees, was trying to pry open a floor safe with a screwdriver. She was wearing a wig, and the long black hair hung halfway to her waist. Marti saw a gun on the floor.

"Don't move."

Linda jumped, then went for the gun. Marti tackled her, heard Linda grunt as she sprawled on top of her, holding her face down. She didn't know where the gun was, and used her weight to keep Linda immobile. Vik rushed over to them.

"Don't move yet, Marti. I've got control of the gun."

Linda gasped at Vik. "My wrist, get off my wrist."

Vik recovered the weapon before he moved his foot.

40

On Sunday morning, Marti drove up to the cabin in Wisconsin where Theo was staying. She left home a little before daybreak, driving Johnny's Bel Air. Yesterday she and Joanna had gone to the cemetery on the far south side of Chicago. At Marti's request, Johnny's plot was on open land, away from trees and shrubbery, so that there were no reminders of Vietnam. The sun was bright, the wind gentle at the grave. The tombstone, a silvery granite, had one word engraved below his name: PEACE. The earth had settled and was flat, the grass green and close-cropped. The rosebush she had planted, also called "Peace," was in bloom. Johnny's irises were planted on either side, and she had brought more with her.

Joanna, always practical, had gotten out the trowel and begun loosening the earth, digging up small clumps of grass. Marti sat by the gravestone to watch her.

"Your dad always wanted a girl. He was so happy that you looked like me." Joanna had been such a plump little baby, with fat, dimpled hands. And he would sing to her, so softly that at first Marti couldn't figure out what the sound was, and she never did identify the song.

"He sang to you," she said. "When you were small."

"I remember."

"No, you don't. You were too little."

"He used to hum 'You Are My Sunshine' when I was in kindergarten and he was walking me to school."

"He did? I didn't know that."

Something about that was comforting. She hoped Joanna

205

felt comforted too, but Joanna jabbed at the earth as if the memory troubled her.

"And he hummed that in my ear the night he took me to that father-daughter dinner and we danced." Marti had forgotten that.

Joanna scattered moist clay and dirt. "Don't see how anything grows here," she complained. "Dad put in topsoil for the irises at home." She arranged and rearranged the irises without finding any configuration that pleased her. "He planted them in rows, not in circles," she said, sounding annoyed as she fussed with them some more.

Marti left her alone until she threw one of the irises and knelt, watching it skitter across the grass.

"I'm going to the movie with Chris tonight."

"Good."

"No. It's not good." She paused. "I need to talk to Dad," Joanna said fiercely. "I get so mad that he left me."

"So do I," Marti said.

When they got back to Lincoln Prairie, Marti had gone to the nursing home to see Addie Liz, Ruth Price's friend. Joanna asked to come along and they took two quarts of ice cream to share with the elderly lady.

Nursing homes depressed Marti—mostly because she wasn't convinced that all of the residents needed to be there. If Addie Liz could get to the park on her own, surely she could take care of herself well enough to live someplace besides here.

The place was clean, well lit, with lots of sunny windows and flowered curtains. Marti stopped a young male aide with a mohawk haircut and a gold stud in his ear.

"You come to see Miss Addie?" he said. "Hey, that's great. Nobody's come to see her since they brought her here from the hospital."

"But her family—" Marti began.

"She's got a grandnephew," the aide interrupted. "He came

here from California on her birthday a couple years back and sends her a package every month or so."

"But the oranges . . ."

"Yeah, she likes them. She used to have one of us bring her a couple every Thursday morning. She hasn't done that in a while, though. We've been kind of worried about her. She seems to have lost her appetite."

"Her friend died," Marti explained. "The one she gave the oranges to."

"Oh." The young man seemed surprised. "That old lady who used to watch TV with her? Too bad. If you just come in here I'll go get her for you."

The sitting room was cheerful too, with lots of hanging plants. The residents were elsewhere, and a large screen television played to empty couches and chairs.

Addie Liz was more stoop-shouldered than Marti remembered, and her dark face seemed more wizened than it had before. The blue shopping bag was strapped to a luggage carrier that she pulled behind her.

"Why, Officer MacAlister."

Marti was surprised that she remembered her name. "Hi, Miss Addie. This is my daughter, Joanna."

"Sure is nice of you to come." She took a closer look at Joanna. "Lord, the child looks like you spit her outta your mouth. I wasn't expectin' no company today. Thought it mighta been one of my grands."

Marti tried not to think about there not being any grands, except for one in California and the grands the old woman made up.

While they ate the ice cream, Addie Liz said, "She died because she saw something she shouldn't have, didn't she? And she didn't know she'd seen anything at all. Never should have asked nobody if that girl died. That's what you get, caring about folks, caring what happens to 'em. Better off not carin' about nobody at all."

"Feels good, having someone care about you," Joanna said. "Even if it does hurt sometimes."

By the time they left, Joanna had promised to come back to see Addie Liz the following week and to give her name to the elderly shut-in program at church. Part of the ambience of living in a smaller city, Marti decided. Easier to get to know people. Too easy to get involved.

Now, as Marti drove toward Wisconsin with the sun rising behind her and the land, hilly with spoon-shaped drumlins, she hummed "You Are My Sunshine." Joanna had gone to the movies with Chris last night. Hallelujah.

Marti didn't take the route with the ferry crossing. The cabin was in a wooded area along the perimeter of Devil's Lake. There were six other cabins along the road, which ended in a cul-de-sac. She missed the place on the first pass. Coming back, she could see the tent pitched behind the cabin and Ben Walker's van parked under some trees.

She wasn't sure why she had come so early, except that she wanted to see these woodlands, a place Theo was so attracted to that was so like a place Johnny never wanted to go near again. It didn't sound like anyone was up yet, and she didn't want to talk with anyone anyway. She peeked into the tent. Both boys were asleep. She walked along a narrow dirt path that wound through the tall trees, and stopped when she reached a ridge that overlooked the tent and the wood-framed cabin.

She sat, shaded by the denseness of oak trees, hedged in by undergrowth, listening to small animal sounds she couldn't identify and birdcalls she hadn't learned yet. She tried not to think for a while, then she tried to superimpose all of the newsreel footage and magazine stills she had seen of the war in Vietnam. She tried to hear gunshots and machine-gun fire and planes overhead and the screams of the dying. She couldn't even imagine what war would be like in a place as serene as these woods.

Then she thought of their trip to the Vietnam Memorial,

watching Johnny find the names of his friends, his eyes wet, Adam's apple bobbing. Johnny had said he didn't understand 'Nam, that none of them did, that they just died or survived. He had survived, to die in another kind of war. But he had found peace again. She was sure that he had.

She heard Theo calling to Mike. "Hey, come look at this toad." She listened for a few minutes as the boys explored the underbrush. "My mother's here," Theo said, noticing the car. Marti headed down to the campsite.

"We have to cook breakfast," Theo called to her. As he spoke, Ben came to the cabin door, looking lean and muscular in T-shirt, camp shorts, and sandals.

"Come on in and have a look around," he said.

The tour took five minutes. "Rustic" was the best way to describe the place. She was surprised that the boys had opted for the tent instead of the loft, which could be reached only by ladder. Ben poured orange juice and they sat outside at the picnic table beneath the wide, interlocking branches of several trees.

"Checking us out?" he asked, smiling.

"Came to see the woods."

"We'll have to go up to the top of the cliff later and look down at the lake. Five hundred feet. Afraid of heights?"

"No."

"Nice here," he said, looking around.

"Peaceful," she agreed.

"Good to get away for a few days."

"Does it remind you of 'Nam?" she asked.

He thought for a minute. "In a way, I suppose. But 'Nam the way it should have been, the way I hope it is now. Those people didn't deserve a war. Who does? Neither did we."

She wondered if Johnny had felt that way, eventually, after that one camping trip, when the nightmares stopped.

"Got your man, huh?" Ben said.

"Man and woman, as it turns out." He must not have seen

a newspaper since they'd left. She filled him in. "Once we locked Linda up, she began bragging about what she had done. Slim was right. She loves an audience. And she has no remorse for killing anyone. Says it was their own fault."

She told him about the floor safe and the screwdriver. "But she seems to have these flashes of intelligence. She got suspicious because the doctor wasn't there the night of the fire. Stole the Martinez girl's key so she could leave through the front door, in case the doctor was watching for her. Then Linda replaced the key with the only one she had, her key to R.D.'s house. We checked. Stupid. Ruth Price was selecting her fruit when R.D. dropped Linda and Janey off in the alley. Even if Ruth hadn't paid attention to that, she might have remembered that Linda exited through the front door, and that she was in such a hurry."

"It's hard to believe that a doctor would set a fire with the intent to kill. Arson to cover up fraud, maybe, but not to murder."

"He was an angry man." She had received Teresa's bank statements from Carmen in yesterday's mail. It would be later in the week before she would have any details, but Teresa had $37,000 in her account. It looked as if she had been asking Edwards for more than a pay increase. That, and Edwards's inability to prevent R.D. and Linda from entering his home whenever they wanted to, had been enough cause for him to act.

"You have to deal with a lot of things that I can avoid," Ben said. "If I fail to resuscitate someone, I don't have to tell their family that they're dead. It must be rough sometimes."

"Sometimes," Marti admitted.

She didn't mention Danny Jones or his sister Virgie. No reason for either of them to be dead, just a terrible chain of events that began when someone fingered Jones for an armed robbery he did not commit. The local African American funeral director was donating his services. She wasn't sure their relatives would attend.

Theo and Mike ran over to the table, laughing. Theo, his

shirt covered with flour, put a Thermos on the picnic table. "Coffee," he said, grinning. Mike gave each of them a plastic mug and took some packets of sugar out of his pocket. Still laughing, the boys ran back to the cabin.

She tasted the hot coffee and added lots of sugar. Ben tasted his and made a face.

"Theo will get the hang of this. He's smart, like his mom. Three perps and you sorted it out." He smiled. "And you've got what you need to make it stick. I'm impressed."

She liked that.

They sipped coffee in a companionable silence until Ben said, "I'm thinking about selling my house when I get back. You sell your place in Chicago?"

"Yes."

"Was it a good move?"

She thought about the spot out front where Johnny had planted his irises. "Don't know," she said. "Just couldn't stay there. For some people staying might be good. I never would have . . ." She paused. "I wouldn't have come to terms with things." She could see that now. "Wouldn't have let the kids, either."

"My place is pretty much like it was when my wife died."

She noticed that he referred to his first wife as "my wife," as if his second wife didn't exist. "And you remarried?" she prompted him, needing to know about that.

He hunched forward, looked down at his mug. "Bad move. Should have sold the house." He shook his head. "We didn't know each other long enough. Didn't want the same things. It was hard on Mike. Shouldn't have done it. Divorce'll be final soon."

"That why you're thinking about selling the house?"

He didn't say anything for a while. "Everything's fine one day, next day they're gone."

"I know."

He looked at her. "Yes, you do," he said. "Crazy time afterwards, isn't it?"

She nodded.

Ben looked past her, at the trees and then over to the house where the boys were fixing breakfast. "Feel like it's time to look ahead now. Maybe that's why I want to sell the house."

The back door burst open. "Breakfast's ready," Theo called. The boys came toward them holding foil-covered plates in their hands. Mike had a bottle of syrup tucked under one arm. Marti peeked under the foil. Thin pancakes, not burned, but really brown. Eggs, fried and crisp around the edges.

The boys looked at each other, said "butter" in unison, and ran back to the cabin.

Mike brought the butter. Theo returned holding a one-gallon terrarium with the three pinecones inside. He had re-created the woods.

"Peace," he said. "No war. The way Dad would have liked it."

Peace. No guns. No war. "Yes, it is the way he would have liked it. The way it is for him now, Theo. The way it is for him now."

Theo grinned and gave her a kiss, then ran off with Mike. Marti looked at the terrarium. "Theo's never cooked breakfast before."

"Mike neither." He tasted a pancake. "Not bad for a start."

Marti looked at him, then at the two boys just reaching the cabin door. "Not bad for a start," she agreed, and covered her pancakes with syrup.